LOVE IS HELL

# LOVE IS
## *Hell*

MELISSA MARR

SCOTT WESTERFELD

JUSTINE LARBALESTIER

GABRIELLE ZEVIN

LAURIE FARIA STOLARZ

HarperCollins *Children's Books*

First published in the USA by HarperCollins *Publishers* 2008
First published in Great Britain by HarperCollins *Children's Books* 2009
HarperCollins *Children's Books* is a division of HarperCollins*Publishers* Ltd,
77-85 Fulham Palace Road, Hammersmith, London W6 8JB

The HarperCollins *Children's Books* website address is
www.harpercollins.co.uk

1

Love is Hell

ISBN-13 978 0 00 734174 0

Printed and bound in England by
Clays Ltd, St Ives plc

**Mixed Sources**
Product group from well-managed
forests and other controlled sources
www.fsc.org  Cert no. SW-COC-1806
FSC  © 1996 Forest Stewardship Council

FSC is a non-profit international organisation established to promote the
responsible management of the world's forests. Products carrying the FSC
label are independently certified to assure consumers that they come
from forests that are managed to meet the social, economic and
ecological needs of present and future generations.

Find out more about HarperCollins and the environment at
www.harpercollins.co.uk/green

**COLLEGESUMMIT.**

LET TALENT SHINE

A portion of the proceeds from the sale of this collection will be donated to College Summit, a national nonprofit organization that partners with school districts to increase the college enrollment rate of all students, particularly those from low-income backgrounds.

### ABOUT COLLEGE ACCESS IN AMERICA

- Every year, 200,000 students who have the ability to go to college do not enroll.
- Low-income students who get As on standardized tests go to college at the same rate as the top-income students who get Ds.

### WHAT COLLEGE SUMMIT IS DOING
### TO HELP SEND MORE STUDENTS TO COLLEGE

College Summit believes that sending one young person to college improves his or her life; sending a group of young people to college can improve a community; but making the college-going process work for all young people can transform our nation.

Since 1993, College Summit has reached more than 35,000 students and trained more than 700 high school teachers in college application management. Additionally, 79% of high school juniors who attend a College Summit workshop enroll in college, nearly double the national average of 46% for low-income high school graduates—an achievement that helps these students break the cycle of poverty in their families forever.

To learn more about College Summit, and for tips on what you can do to prepare yourself for college or encourage others, visit www.collegesummit.org.

# Sleeping
## with the
# Spirit

## LAURIE FARIA
## STOLARZ

# One

J WAKE UP IN a cold sweat—a sharp, biting sensation stretches down the length of my spine and makes my fingers jitter. I pull the covers around my shoulders, feeling my heart beat fast.

And noticing the ache in my wrist.

I click the reading lamp on and look down at the spot. Another soon-to-be bruise—a giant red welt that covers the front of my wrist and wraps around to the underside. So I grab the pen on my bedside table and add another point to the tally I've been keeping for the past two weeks since we moved here—to mark the sixth time this has happened.

*Six* times.

Six times that I've woken up with a sore spot on my body.

Six times that I've found myself lying awake in my bed, too terrified to fall back asleep.

Because of the voice that haunts my dreams.

Ever since we moved here, I've been having these weird nightmares. In them, I hear a male voice. I never see his face. It's just his voice, whispering things that I don't want to hear—that ghosts exist, that I need to listen to him, that he won't let me rest until I do.

Luckily, I'm able to force myself awake. But that's when he grips me—so hard that it leaves a mark.

I know it sounds completely crazy and at first I tried to find some logical explanation—maybe I had twisted my arm the wrong way during the night; maybe I had banged my leg on the corner of my bed or rolled over into an awkward position.

I tried to tell myself that the dreams were the result of stress—of having to move halfway across the country; of changing high schools and leaving all my friends behind. I mean, there's bound to be a period of adjustment, right?

But now I know that it's more than stress. Because, between the bruising and the aching, and the growing sacks underneath my eyes from lack of sleep, I feel like things are getting worse.

"Brenda?" my mother asks, standing by my bedroom door. "What are you doing up?"

I bury my wrist in the mound of covers, noticing how

the smell of him—like spiced apple—still lingers in my sheets.

"You were moaning in your sleep," she continues.

I glance at the fire-red numbers glowing on my digital clock. It's 4:05 A.M. "A bad dream, I guess," I say, trying to shrug it off.

She nods and plays with the belt on her robe, just lingering there in the doorway, until she finally ventures the question: "You're not hearing voices again, are you?"

I study her face, wondering if she can handle the answer, but decide that she can't. So I shake my head, watching her expression shift from anxiety to relief. She lets out a breath and forces a smile, still fidgeting with her robe, probably wondering about my sanity.

But that's okay.

Because I wonder about it, too.

This isn't the first time my parents have found me awake in the wee hours of the morning. This isn't the first time they've complained about the moaning, or given me that frightened look—the one that says I'm going crazy.

Or noticed all my bruises.

The first time I got one it was around my ankle—a large purple splotch, lined with a handful of scratches. The night it happened, I went to their room, asking if they could hear the voice, too, wondering if maybe someone had broken into our house—if maybe the voice wasn't part of a dream at all.

But my parents said no, they hadn't heard anything. They looked particularly concerned after my father had checked things out, upon my insistence, like they were far more scared *for* me than *with* me.

"Do you want me to fix you some warm milk?" my mother asks now.

"No thanks," I say, still able to hear the voice from my dream. It plays in my mind's ear—a slow and rhythmic breath that pushes out the two syllables of my name over and over and over again: *Bren-da, Bren-da, Bren-da.*

"I just want to get back to sleep," I lie, catching a glimpse of myself in the dresser mirror. My normally bright green eyes are troubled with veins of red. And my hair is a mess—an unruly tangle of auburn curls swooped high atop my head in a sloppy ponytail, because I can't deal with actually having to style the high-maintenance mane.

Because I haven't gotten a full night's sleep since we moved here.

"Good night, Mom," I whisper, and lie back on my pillow to appease her, so she'll go back to bed. I pull the covers up over my ears and silently hum a little tune inside my head, in hopes that it will calm me down.

In hopes that it will drown out his voice.

# Two

THE FOLLOWING DAY AT school, Monsieur DuBois, my French teacher, pairs us all up to do a role-playing exercise. I've dubbed myself Isabelle, while Raina, my partner, is Marie-Claire. We begin by chatting about our hobbies and school schedules and then, when Monsieur seems far too preoccupied as he hangs pictures on the wall of various types of French cheese—and Raina and I have reached the limits of our French vocabulary—she tells me (in English) that last year, mid-December, right before the sophomore semiformal, she was the new kid, too.

"It seriously sucks having to leave your whole life behind," she says, weaving her espresso-dark hair into a long, thick braid at the side of her head.

I nod, thinking about my friends back home,

wondering what they're doing right now.

And if they're missing me, too.

"So, I notice you haven't really been hanging with anyone," Raina continues. "I saw you sitting by yourself in the cafeteria the other day. That's social suicide, you know. If left untreated, it can lead to social roadkill."

"Roadkill?"

She nods, still braiding her hair, trying to get all the layers woven in, despite the plethora of barrettes she's got adorning the top of her head. "It's a killer for the social life—sets you up for the rest of your high school career, especially being midyear, you know. Everybody's already cliqued-off."

"Cliqued-off?"

"Yeah," she says, her brown eyes bulging slightly like it comes as a big, fat shock that I don't quite get her lingo—especially since we're both supposedly speaking in our native tongue now. "Everybody's already settled into their cliques," she explains. "People will see you as a loner. I mean, unless you *want* to be alone. . . ."

"I hadn't exactly given it much thought."

"Well, you *should*," she says. "Because there isn't much time."

I feel my face scrunch, as clueless to her philosophy as I am to her vocabulary.

"Want *my* opinion?" she asks.

I open my mouth to switch the subject, to ask about

the next homework assignment, but then Raina gives me her opinion anyway: "Why sulk about a bad move to East Bum Suck, Massachusetts, a whole hour and twelve minutes' drive from Boston . . . ? On a *good* day, that is. Bottom line: You should totally hang out with Craig and me."

At the same moment, a boy with brown spiky hair and a freckly face, who I presume to be Craig, swivels around in his seat. "Did somebody call?"

"Craig, Brenda; Brenda, Craig," she says to introduce us.

"Enchanté," Craig says, faking a French accent. "But the name's Jean-Claude until the bell rings."

Raina rolls her eyes and then gives Craig the lowdown on my "situation," turning my new-kid status into a sociological diagnosis. According to her, I've only got another week, tops, to bounce back from my loner status before I'm permanently branded a dweeb.

"Don't mind Raina," Craig says, clearly sensing my discomfort. "She tends to get a little carried away by social politics."

"*Whatever* . . ." Raina says, wrapping a rubber band around the end of her braid, having finally gotten it just so. "You know I'm totally right."

Craig shrugs and focuses back on me. "So, what do you say? Table for *trois*, starting tomorrow?"

"You're such a cheese-ass," Raina says, undoubtedly referring to his French.

"Sounds good." I smile, confident that this is the first time I've felt somewhat normal since I moved here.

# Three

I'M IN MY ROOM when the clock downstairs bongs 11:00 P.M., but I don't want to go to sleep. I run my fingers over my wrist, noticing how the red mark has morphed into a deep shade of purple, and how the knot in my stomach gets bigger with each chime.

I've done all my homework, taken my shower, and alphabetized all the books on my shelf, trying my hardest to stay awake, but after an infomercial on butt-lifting pantyhose, a mini-marathon of *Cops*, and more than an hour of QVC jewelry, I feel myself start to doze.

Until I hear a knock on my door.

"Come in," I call, assuming it's my mother. She often likes to check in on me at night.

But the door doesn't open.

I sit up in bed and click on the bedside lamp.

"Mom . . . is that you?"

No one answers.

I let out a sigh and get up and move toward the door. I try the knob, but it doesn't budge, like I've been locked inside.

"Mom?" I repeat, still trying to get the knob to turn. I pound on the door, hoping to get my parents' attention down the hall.

But no one comes. And the knob won't turn.

"Brenda," a voice whispers from somewhere behind me. *His* voice—the one from my dreams.

I turn to look, my heart pumping hard.

"Are you ready to talk?" his voice continues.

I glance around the room, but I don't see him anywhere. Meanwhile everything looks different now. My bed is draped in navy blue linens rather than the pinks from just moments ago. And the swimming and field hockey plaques that hung on my walls—the ones I've won over the past five years—have been replaced by Bruins memorabilia: flags, hockey sticks, and posters.

I shake my head, wondering where I am, knowing that this isn't my room.

And that I shouldn't be here.

"We need to talk," his voice whispers. I can feel his breath at the back of my neck.

I whirl around and try to swipe him away, but no one's there. And then the lamp by my bed goes out, leaving me in complete darkness.

A moment later, the moon casts a strip of light through my window, illuminating a corner of the room where a shadow moves along the wall.

I go for the door again. I pound and kick against it, then yank the knob with all my might.

But nothing works.

"Don't be afraid," he says, stepping into the moonlight, and allowing me to see him—his pale blue eyes and the curl of his mouth. He must be my age, maybe seventeen or eighteen at most, with at least five inches of height over me, and hair the color of cashews.

As he moves closer, a shadow lifts from his brow, revealing a gash in his forehead, like he's been hit with something. The wound is fresh and deep.

"My name is Travis," he says. "And I've waited so long for someone like you."

Dressed all in black, from the T-shirt that hugs his chest to the rubber-soled boots adorning his feet, he stares at me—hard—his eyes refusing to blink.

"Someone like me?" I ask.

He nods and moves a little closer. "Someone who can see and hear me. I've been waiting so long to be heard."

I try to take another step back, but between him and the door I'm completely trapped.

"I'm sorry about your wrist." He reaches out to touch it, but I snatch my hand away before he can. "I didn't mean to hurt you," he continues. "I was only trying to hold on to you, so you wouldn't leave your dream by waking up." He takes another step, only inches from me now. "It's rough for us ghosts. We don't know the power of our own strength, especially when we're trying to make physical contact with those who aren't asleep, or, like you, who are on the verge of waking up. It's all about frequency and energy. Very complicated stuff." He smiles.

I shake my head and struggle to wake up. I think he must sense it, because a moment later, he clenches around my forearm.

"Please," he urges, his face all serious. "Don't leave me tonight."

"No!" I shout, pulling away.

He tries to grab my arm back, but my scream wakes me up.

"Brenda?" my dad asks, throwing open my bedroom door.

I sit up in bed and try to catch my breath, noting how everything in my room looks normal again—my pink bedcovers and plaques on the wall.

"Are you okay?" He checks around the room.

I try my best to nod, even though I feel anything but okay—even though a warm and tingling sensation still lingers in my forearm.

# Four

AT LUNCH THE FOLLOWING day, instead of sitting by myself, I'm flagged down by Raina and Craig, which is definitely a blessing. Social roadkill aside, I'm in serious need of a diversion. I just can't stop thinking about my dream last night.

I wish there were someone I could talk to about everything, but it's sort of like when my sister died. I tried to explain what I felt then, too—what I *knew* had happened—but no one understood.

And how could they?

How can anyone make sense of something so non-sensical: the sight of my sister, Emma, in her Girl Scout uniform—the one she always insisted on wearing to bake sales, cookie sales, troop meetings, or just around the house. She'd been in a coma for six full months.

But I still saw her that day. She opened the front door of our house, crossed the living room to kiss me good-bye, and then vanished without a word.

I knew it was her ghost that appeared to me. I knew that she had died. When I tried to tell my mother, she buckled to the ground, refusing to believe me, telling me I was cruel and insensitive for making up such horrible lies. But then, not even five minutes later, my father called from the hospital and told us—Emma had passed away.

Craig slides a bowl full of crinkle fries and ranch dressing toward me. "How's it going?" he asks.

Raina frowns at the offering. "You really want to nauseate the girl on her first day of lunching with us?"

"Actually," I say, "this looks great."

Craig seems to like the answer. His smile grows wide, showing off the tiny—yet adorable—gap between his two front teeth. "I *knew* this girl had taste."

We end up trading lunches like in grammar school—a few of his fries for a couple of my peanut butter–stuffed celery sticks. And then Craig suggests that we all get together this weekend. "Raina and I can give you a tour of the town," he says.

"Should take all of five minutes," Raina jokes, glancing at the bruise on my wrist.

I tug my sleeve down to cover it over, and then give them a thumbs-up for the tour. We end up making plans for Saturday night—at 7:00 P.M. sharp. Craig offers to come pick me up, and that's when I tell them my address.

"*Are you kidding?*" Raina gasps, nearly snorting out her strawberry milk. "The bloodbath house?"

"What are you talking about?" I pause mid-chew.

"No big deal," Craig says, trying to make light of it. "Just your typical friendly neighborhood—"

"*Bloodbath!*" Raina bursts out, finishing for him. "Didn't the real estate agent tell you the history of your house?"

I shake my head as they give me the details: a seventeen-year-old boy was murdered there, the police found his body in the bathroom, and it was the mother's boyfriend who did it.

"Apparently, a blow to the head," Craig explains. "The boyfriend hit him with a crowbar and he landed hard against the cast-iron tub."

"Hence the bath of blood," Raina offers.

"Lovely," I say, thinking about the boy in my dream— he had a gash in his forehead.

"Seriously," Raina continues, "I don't even know how you can sleep at night. People say the place is crazy-haunted."

"I *can't* sleep at night," I say, feeling my stomach churn. "I mean, not usually."

"Well, that would explain it," she says. "I mean, I

hate to be rude, but you're packin' some serious baggage under those peepers, and I'm not exactly talking Louis Vuitton."

"Nope, not rude at all." Craig sighs.

Raina hands me a stick of cover-up, explaining that it's "the good stuff," reserved only for after her late-night study marathons.

"Which is why it's never been used," Craig clarifies.

While they continue to bicker, I slide back in my chair, fighting the urge to toss up my french fries right on the spot.

"Are you okay?" Craig asks, probably noticing the sickly look on my face.

"Yeah," Raina jokes, "your head isn't going to do a three-sixty on us, is it? All I need right now is a hunk of spew to land in my duck sauce."

"I have to go," I say, getting up from the table. I grab my books and bolt out of the cafeteria, foregoing Raina's stick of cover-up, since it's obviously going to take a whole lot more than makeup to fix what's going on inside my house.

And in my dreams.

# Five

As soon as I get home from school, I dump my books on the floor and make a beeline for my computer. I begin by Googling our home address, which is actually all it takes. An article from the *Addison Gazette* pops up right away.

It's all about our house, about how it finally sold—to my parents—after years of sitting on the market. Apparently we're not the first family to live here since the infamous bloodbath. Two other families inhabited this place, but it didn't take them long to bolt—six months for the first family, six years for the second. Both claimed that things went bump in the night.

The article segues into the history of the house, and what happened here twenty years ago. Raina and Craig were right. A seventeen-year-old boy was murdered. His body was found in the bathtub after he'd been hit over the head with a crowbar.

"Travis Slather," I whisper, reading the victim's name aloud. A toxic taste lines the inside of my mouth. I close my eyes, trying to hold it all together, remembering the boy in my dream last night.

He told me his name was Travis.

According to the article, Jocelyn, Travis's mother, was home when it happened, but she'd been badly beaten herself. The police discovered her huddled inside the hallway closet downstairs, barely still alive. I read on, learning tidbits about the killer—that he was indeed the mother's boyfriend, that he had a criminal record filled with domestic abuse offenses, and that he's currently serving a life sentence in prison.

I glance over my shoulder at my room, conjuring up the images from my dream—the Bruins gear and the navy blue bedcovers—knowing somehow that this was *his* room, which prompts me to search even more.

I end up navigating to a site called "New England's Most Haunted Homes." I scroll down to a picture of my house. It basically looks the same as it does now—same brown color, same wooden steps, same black metal mailbox—except the maple tree in the front is much taller now. And the window on the second floor—the one in my bedroom—is no longer boarded up.

It seriously gives me chills.

I try a bunch of other sites, looking for information about ghosts and hauntings, weeding through all the individual posts—from those claiming to have the likes of Elvis, Marilyn Monroe, and Kurt Cobain taking over their bodies—until I finally find something worthwhile.

It's a website that talks about hauntings in general, stating that ghosts who haunt tend to do so because they can't pass on, because they have some unfinished business to attend to. They cling to people who have some sort of extrasensory insight, relying on them to tie up their loose ends.

So they can finally rest at last.

A tight little knot forms in my chest just thinking about it. I mean, aside from that one time with Emma, I've never really thought of myself as being or having anything extra-*anything*, never mind possessing supernatural powers.

"Brenda?" my dad calls, edging open my bedroom door. "Are you okay? You've been in here all afternoon. I thought maybe we could watch the game together."

"Why didn't you guys tell me?" I say, trying my best not to hyperventilate.

He opens the door wide. "Tell you *what*?"

"That this place is haunted, that a boy was murdered here twenty years ago."

"Since when do you believe in ghosts?"

"Since Emma died," I say, feeling my jaw stiffen.

He glances down the hallway, checking to make sure my mother's out of earshot. "Dinner's in a half hour," he says in a lame-o attempt to ignore me.

It's an unspoken rule in our family that we're not allowed to talk about Emma. Ever since she died five years ago, it's almost as if she'd never existed. My parents hired movers to come and clean out her bedroom and turn the space into a home office—an office that no one ever used. Meanwhile, my mother dove headfirst into her work at the candy factory, taking any and all shifts she could get, so she wouldn't have to think. Or spend time at home. So everything would just go numb.

It's gotten a little better over the years, but my mother's never really been the same.

And I suppose I haven't been, either.

Part of me blames myself for Emma's accident. She had asked to borrow my roller skates that day so that she could practice her spins in the driveway. But I said no. And so Emma ended up going for a bike ride instead. She rode by herself to the park and crossed a main intersection without looking twice.

She never came home.

"I asked you a question," I say, staring hard at the side of his face. My father refuses to meet my eye.

"This is a good house with good people in it," he says, talking to the wall. "End of story."

"It's *not* the end." I shake my head. "Why didn't you

tell me? Didn't you think I'd find out anyway?"

"We don't believe in ghosts," he snaps.

"No," I say, biting back. "*You* don't."

"Dinner's in a half hour," he repeats, pulling the door closed behind him.

I tell him I'm not hungry, but I don't think he hears me.

Because he's already left the room.

# *Six*

*U*NWILLING TO FALL ASLEEP last night, I burned
away the hours doing more online research.

And learning more about Travis.

About his love for hockey and all things Bruins; how
he loved to go camping, even in cold weather. And how
he had to deal with a major loss, too.

His father died of heart failure when Travis was only
seven, leaving Travis completely devastated.

The whole idea of it—of how human Travis sounds in
news articles and testimonials, and how it seems we had
a few things in common—keeps me awake through all
of my classes, my mind whirling with questions.

But, now, at the end of the school day, I'm beyond
exhausted. Even the cracked vinyl seats in the bus feel

cozy. I sink down into one near the back and stare out the window, waiting for the driver to finally reach my stop.

And that's when I feel something brush against my shoulder. I turn to look.

It's him, sitting in the seat behind me—*Travis*.

"Hello, Brenda." His pale blue eyes are fixed on mine. The gash in his forehead is no longer there.

My mouth trembles open, surprised at how good he looks, at the broadness of his shoulders and the intensity of his stare. I look away, wondering if anyone else can see him, but it appears that we're alone, that all the other kids have already been let off at their stops.

He leans forward and rests his hand on the back of my seat, revealing the muscles in his forearm and the scar on his thumb. "You've been doing some research about me," he says.

I manage a nod and slide my hand away, afraid he'll try to grab it, like in my dreams.

"Have you found what you were looking for?" he continues.

I shake my head, knowing that I haven't. When Emma appeared to me that day, she had one goal in mind: to say goodbye. I have no idea what Travis's goal is.

"What do you want?" I ask, wondering how this is even possible, how he's even sitting here right now.

He smiles as though amused by my confusion. "First,"

he says, leaning in even closer, "what I *don't* want is to hurt you. But I *do* need your help." His hand glides along the back of my seat, just inches from mine again. "I can't force you to stay with me in your dreams; it obviously doesn't work and I was stupid to even try." He glances at my wrist. "The truth is I need you to *want* to stay with me, to *want* to help me and hear me out. I won't be able to rest until you do."

I take a deep breath, thinking about my sister, Emma. In some ways, I'm not at rest, either.

Travis swallows hard, continuing to study me. "I could help you, too, you know."

"I don't need any help," I say, my voice quavering over the words.

"Not at all?"

I glance away, avoiding the question, feeling the heat of his breath at my chin. He smells like baked apples.

A second later, the bus pulls up to my stop.

Travis moves his hand so that it rests on top of mine, making my heart thrash around inside my chest.

"Will you help me?" he asks.

My lip quivers, noting his urgent tone. Part of me wants to tell him yes; another part wants to wake up out of this dream and never sleep again.

"Getting out?" the bus driver asks.

I meet Travis's eye, watching him watch me, focusing a moment on his full, pale lips and the tension in his jaw.

"Hel-looooo?" the driver shouts.

A moment later, I feel my body being shook. I reluctantly open my eyes, only to find some blond-haired girl with huge green glasses standing right over me, trying to shake me awake. Everyone on the bus turns to look at me—there are at least twenty kids. The bus driver glares in my direction from his rearview mirror. "Getting out?" he repeats.

I nod, grab my book, and then scurry out the door.

# Seven

*LATER,* AT HOME, I struggle to fall asleep, to pick up where my last dream left off, but my visit from Travis has left me more mentally awake than ever. Even though, physically, I'm beyond exhausted.

At breakfast the following morning, my mother serves me a heaping stack of pancakes, insisting that I need to eat, and that my pale complexion and bloodshot eyes have her and my dad worried. But after a night of maybe two hours of sleep tops, I have no appetite, and so I end up making roads in the pool of maple syrup on my plate, unable to get my mind off Travis.

And unable to stay awake.

Finally, after three bites and a good fifteen minutes of maple syrup tracks, I excuse myself from the table and head upstairs to the bathroom. I close and lock the door behind me, feeling a chill pass over my shoulders.

It's not like I haven't been in here before. It's just that ever since I learned about what happened in this house, I've been avoiding it like the proverbial plague, opting instead for the bathroom downstairs.

I glance around, wondering what it looked like twenty years ago. Were the walls butter-colored like now? Are these the same ceramic floor tiles? The same chrome-plated sink faucet?

And what about the tub?

I look down at it, my heart pounding so loud I can almost hear it in my ears. Images of that day from twenty years ago flash across my mind—even though I wasn't here; I hadn't even been born yet. I can picture Travis's face and the look of surprise when the crowbar came at him. And I can see him falling back, headfirst, against the bottom of the cast-iron tub.

I turn away, resisting the urge to be sick and noticing how cold I feel. The temperature in the room must have dropped at least ten degrees.

"Brenda?" my mother calls out, knocking on the door. "Are you okay?"

"Fine," I say, zooming in on the radiator beneath the window, wondering if it's working right.

"Do you want more pancakes?" she asks.

I tell her I don't, baffled that she would even ask. I

mean, did she not notice my unfinished plate?

I move across the room to check the heat, holding my palms out by the radiator. But all I feel is coldness—a sharp penetrating chill that crawls over my bones and makes my skin itch.

At the same moment, something touches my back and snakes up my spine. Startled, I turn to look. But no one's there—no one's by the sink or in the tub, even though it feels like someone's watching me.

"Mom?" I call, wondering if she's still outside the door.

She doesn't answer.

I turn back around, telling myself that it's just my imagination and that I need to get a grip.

The rungs of the radiator are as frigid as the room. I squat down and place my ear up against them. I want to see if I can hear the rush of heat rising up through the pipes, but it's eerily quiet.

A moment later, I spot something shiny between the rungs. It looks like a chain of some sort, maybe a necklace. I try sticking my fingers in to retrieve it, but the chain is several inches away.

"Brenda," my mother calls, from behind the door again.

I take a deep breath. The smell of mulled apples is thick in the air. "Travis?" I whisper.

"Brenda," my mother repeats. "Get up NOW!" She

smacks something hard near my head. The impact of the noise wakes me up.

I'm no longer in the bathroom. I'm in the kitchen, at the table, and my head rests on a pillow of napkins. There's a plateful of pancakes in front of me. "I'm sorry," I say, sitting up straight. My mother is standing over me, a fry pan clutched in her hand—obviously what she used to wake me up. "I must have fallen asleep."

"Your father and I are really worried about you," she reminds me.

"I'm sorry," I repeat.

"Are you using drugs?" Her mouth is a thin, angry line.

I shake my head, too tired to even entertain her stupid theory. Instead, I grab my butter knife, excuse myself from the table—for *real* this time—and head straight for the upstairs bathroom.

The cast-iron radiator is in full view. Just like in my dream, it's been painted a metallic silver, but you can still see the hunter green shade underneath where the paint has chipped in spots. I approach it slowly, noting the chill in the room, feeling the gooseflesh sprout up on my arms. I squat down and peek between the rungs.

And that's when I see it—the necklace from my dreams.

"Brenda?" my mother asks, pushing the door wide. "What's the matter?"

My mouth trembles open, but no words come out.

Her eyes narrow, spotting the knife in my hand. "What are you doing?"

"I dropped my necklace," I say, finally.

She nods, but I can tell she doesn't quite believe me. Still, she leaves me alone, commenting on the chill in the room and on how she needs to check the thermostat downstairs.

It takes some maneuvering, but I'm able to work the necklace out from the rungs using the butter knife.

It's a sterling-silver chain with a heart-shaped pendant. I glide my fingers down the length, noticing how the clasp is still fastened but the links have been broken. The initials JAS are engraved across the pendant's surface in pretty cursive writing.

My heart speeds up, conjuring up all those online articles. Mrs. Slather's first name is Jocelyn.

This must belong to her.

# Eight

SATURDAY NIGHT, CRAIG AND Raina take me on a tour of the town, which consists of driving by the ice cream/pizza place on Main Street, the barbershop where Craig gets his hair cut, and a corner grocery that sells everything from garden rakes to garden vegetables. Our last stop is a coffee shop, which, according to Raina, is the least lamest place in town.

Ever-exhausted, I order a double espresso with an extra shot.

"Are you kidding?" Raina squawks. "The sign on the door says *Stanley's*, not Starbucks. It's one coffee bean fits all here."

We each end up with a cup of regular, and then Raina leads us to a booth in the corner.

"So, what's up with the need for speed?" she asks.

"Excuse me?"

"A *double espresso with an extra shot*?" She raises her stud-pierced eyebrow in curiosity. "I thought the problem was that you *couldn't* sleep. With rocket fuel like that, I'd be doing jumping jacks around my bedroom all night."

"Now there's a sobering sight," Craig says.

I take a sip of my less-than-palatable cup of java, knowing full well that I *do* want to sleep, but a part of me is still afraid of what I'll see, of what it'll mean. And, yet, ever since my dream on the bus the other day, since I've been doing all this research and learning about Travis, I can't help but wonder if I'll see him again.

If he'll clasp my hand.

And make my heart race.

"Is it getting easier, at least?" Craig asks. "To sleep in the new place, I mean."

I shrug, thinking about the necklace I found. I've hidden it inside an old tennis sneaker at the back of my closet, right beside my roller skates—the ones I didn't let Emma borrow.

Even though they're at least three sizes too small now, I've been keeping the skates ever since that day, unable to let go of what happened.

"I was talking to my folks about your house," Craig continues. "Talk about townies . . . my parents have both lived here since birth. But the whole murder story . . . it's actually a lot sadder than I thought."

"Sadder than a bloody bathtub?" Raina asks.

Craig nods. "Turns out Travis was actually trying to spare his mother a serious beating that day. Apparently, he came home and saw his mom's boyfriend going at her with his fist. Travis tried to distract the guy by using himself as beating bait. When his mother went to call 911, she couldn't get the words out. She was too scared of what the boyfriend would do to her, I guess. She ended up hiding away in the downstairs closet because she couldn't stand hearing the crap getting kicked out of her son."

"Sounds like a nice lady," Raina says.

Craig shrugs. "I guess she pretty much lost it after that. She blamed herself. At least that's what people say."

"Where is she now?" I ask.

"She's a townie, too," he says. "She lives in one of the condos behind the lake. At least that's what my parents tell me."

"Better watch out." Raina smirks. "You're starting to sound like a townie yourself."

"Better to sound like one than to look like one," he says, gesturing to her sweatshirt. There's a giant shark, the school's mascot, swimming above the words "Addison High Bites."

"I dream about him," I blurt out, putting an end to their banter.

"You dream about *who*?" Raina asks.

"Travis Slather."

"Um, what are you talking about?" Craig asks.

I take a giant breath and tell them everything: how it started with just his voice; how I'd wake up with unexplained bruises; and then how he appeared to me recently, asking for my help.

"I told you that place was crazy-haunted," Raina says.

"But maybe you're dreaming about him because of everything you've heard," Craig says. "I mean, I'd probably be having nightmares, too."

"No way," I say. "I started dreaming about him before I even knew about the murder, before I knew the house was supposedly haunted."

"So, how are you supposed to help him?" he asks.

"I don't know." I shake my head.

"Well, is he hot at least?" Raina sighs. "Because I heard the boy was hot."

"Here we go." Craig rolls his eyes.

But I can't help smiling at her remark. I try my best to stop it, but the grin inches up my face and warms my cheeks.

Because the boy *is* hot.

Because a part of me can't wait to see him again.

# Nine

IN MY ROOM, I change into my pajamas—an oversized Bruins T-shirt coupled with a pair of flannel shorts—and guzzle down a full glass of sleep-inducing warm milk. Before I get into bed, I open my window, allowing the cool, fresh breeze to filter into the room.

The sky looks amazing tonight with its swollen moon and sprinkling of stars. I edge the curtains open wider, trying my best to relax my mind by thinking about simple things, like tomorrow's hockey game and cinnamon toast for breakfast, but my pulse races and my head feels all dizzy.

Because all I can think about is Travis.

I take a deep breath and then exhale for five full seconds, trying to thwack myself out of it, but when I turn around, he's sitting there on the corner of my bed.

"Hello, Brenda," Travis says. "You've been waiting for me, haven't you?"

I nod. My face flashes hot.

"Good, because I've been waiting for you, too." He stands and extends his hand to me.

I take it and we both just sort of stand there, staring at each other. "I want to help you," I say, noting the warmth of his palm.

"Are you sure?"

I nod again and glance up at his forehead where the gash used to be.

"It's still there," he says, rubbing the spot. "But it isn't exactly pretty, so I've sort of hidden it away—one of the perks of being a ghost." He smiles, trying to make light of it.

"Does it still hurt?"

He nods, sandwiching my hands between his palms and turning my insides to absolute mush. "It won't heal until I do."

"Hold that thought," I say, eager to show him the necklace. I move over to the closet and swing the door wide.

My roller skates are in full view.

I take a step back, my hands trembling. My mouth turns dry. Normally, I keep the skates in a brown paper bag, tucked behind a suitcase in the very back.

"How did these get here?" I whisper.

"Brenda?" Travis asks. "Are you okay?"

I shake my head, wondering how this could possibly happen. Did my mother rearrange my closet when I wasn't home? Was my dad snooping around in here?

Travis comes and wraps his arms around my shoulders from behind. "They're just skates," he says.

"No," I say, feeling my eyes well up. "You don't understand."

"I do," he whispers. "I understand a whole lot more than you think. And they're just skates. They're not *her*. They shouldn't represent her."

"Did you do this?" I ask, turning toward him.

"Don't be upset." He wipes my tears with the corner of his sleeve. "I just want you to be happy. Your sister would want that, too. And you can't be happy when you're trying to hide the past in a paper bag. Think about the good times you had with your sister when you want to remember her. Don't think about these skates."

"How do *you* know what my sister wants?"

"I think I speak from experience," he says.

I want to be mad at him, but I can't. And as messed up as it sounds, it feels really good to cry. After Emma died, I wasn't allowed to show even a speck of emotion, and now it seems too big to hold back.

Travis holds me for way longer than anyone else ever has, until all my Emma tears have dried up.

"Thanks," I say, wiping my eyes, trying to regain composure.

"Sure." He smiles and reaches for my hand, gives it a squeeze, then moves past me to go into the closet. He pulls the necklace from my old tennis shoe. "I watched you hide it in here," he says. "I gave this to my mom on Mother's Day. I still remember that morning. I had tried to make French toast, but it turned out to be more like soggy bagel bites. We ended up eating cornflakes." He laughs and runs his thumb over the heart-shaped pendant. "Anyway, I gave this to her, along with a bouquet of wildflowers. The day I was killed, that bastard ripped it off her neck and chucked it across the bathroom. It landed in the radiator, but she was never able to find it."

"I'm sorry about what happened to you."

He shrugs. "That's life, I guess. There are no guarantees. Like with my dad . . . as far as everyone knew, he was in perfect health. But, then, one day, he just never came home."

I nod, thinking how it was like that with Emma, too. "Did you enjoy your life at least?"

"It had its moments." He smiles again and his eyes lock on mine. "I only have one regret."

"Which is?"

"Not living long enough to tell my mother that what happened wasn't her fault. I stepped in to help her—to distract that asshole from beating her—because I wanted to. It was my choice."

"But you were only seventeen."

"I know."

"And you aren't angry at all?"

He shrugs again. "What good would that do? My mother did the best she could, but she wasn't a strong woman. I knew that. Her boyfriend knew it, too. That's why he beat her down so bad. Plus, you could totally turn things around and say it was my fault. If my mother was too weak to do the right thing, maybe I should have reported him long before anything like that ever happened."

"I guess," I say, wondering how he can be so forgiving.

"Besides," he continues, "life's too short to live with all that guilt. That's what my mother's doing now, even twenty years later. And that's what you're doing, too, isn't it . . . with Emma?"

I shrug and look away. "How do you know so much about me?"

"I'm inside your dreams, remember? I know all about you."

I nod, slightly disappointed that *this* is a dream, that I eventually have to wake up.

"So, will you help me?" he asks, dropping the necklace into my palm. "Will you bring this to her? Will you tell her that I don't blame her for my death?"

"And what'll happen then?" I ask.

Travis bites his lip and touches my face. His fingers feel like velvet against my skin. "I'll be able to pass on."

"That's what I thought," I say, hearing the disappointment in my voice.

"But I want to spend more time with you first." He runs his fingers along my jaw. "I want to see you as often as I can before that time comes."

"And when *will* it come?"

He whisks a lock of tear-soaked hair off my face and leans in a little closer, his lips just inches from mine. "Whatever you do," he whispers, ignoring the question, "don't wake up now."

A moment later, I feel his kiss. It presses against my mouth and makes my skin sizzle. "We don't have much time," he says, once the kiss breaks. "You're going to wake up soon. I can sense it."

"So what now?"

"Now I hold you while I still can."

We lay in my bed, Travis cradling me in his embrace. I try to stay asleep, to relish the moment for as long as I can. But the sound of birds chirping outside wakes me up.

I roll over in bed to look for him. His mother's necklace rests on the pillow beside me. But Travis is nowhere in sight.

# Ten

$\mathcal{J}$ SPEND THE NEXT SEVERAL days sleeping when-ever I can—drinking lots of warm milk, switch-ing to decaf, and reducing my intake of sugar, carbs, and anything else that might keep me awake. Raina tells me she can see the difference, but attributes it to her stellar makeup tips and not to the fact that I've been going to bed early each night, taking catnaps during the day.

And seeing Travis.

In my dreams, Travis and I talk about everything—about his favorite '80s flicks (*Back to the Future* and *Ferris Bueller's Day Off*), how I'd like to start swimming again, and how he misses the taste of fudge ripple ice cream. We talk about music we love and places we've visited. And places he never got to see.

We even talk about Emma.

While my parents won't even allow me to say her name, Travis listens as I talk about the day of Emma's accident, the six months that followed while she was in a coma, and the day that she died—when her ghost appeared to me.

"I think about her all the time," I tell him on our last night together. "I wonder what she'd be like now, if we'd be close and if I'd teach her stuff—like how to make butterscotch candy—my culinary specialty—or how to trap and dribble in field hockey. I just hope she's happy . . . wherever she is."

"She is," he says, pulling me close. "There's no need to feel bad about anything."

"Are you sure?"

He breaks our embrace to look at me. He cups my face and stares into my eyes. "More than sure."

"I don't want to lose you," I say, fighting the urge to well up.

"There's still right now," he says. "So, don't wake up."

"I'll do my best."

We end up taking a walk by the lake, where he and his dad used to go fishing. Travis picks a spot close to the water and lays out a thick blanket. We sit down facing one another, holding hands, and entangling legs.

"I wish you could stay," I whisper.

Travis threads his fingers through mine, sending warm and spicy tingles straight down my back. "I'll always be with you," he says.

"But not like now. I won't be able to see you."

"It wouldn't be fair of me to stay. You have your own life to live."

"Well, maybe I want to live it with you."

He smiles and brushes his forehead against mine. And then he kisses me and it tastes like hot apple cider inside my mouth. "I'll always be with you," he repeats, murmuring into my ear. "Just don't ever say goodbye."

I rest my head against his chest as tears drip down the sides of my face.

We continue to hold and kiss each other, until the sun rises up and paints a strip of gold across the water . . . and I wake up.

# Eleven

THE SUN BEAMS THROUGH my bedroom window. I squint against it and roll over in bed, wondering why my alarm clock didn't go off, especially since today is the day I've planned to see Travis's mother.

Around ten, Craig comes to pick me up. He volunteered to take me to Mrs. Slather's condo. Just a few days ago, I told him and Raina the full story—about the necklace, about my sister, Emma, and how my relationship with Travis has gone from zero to sixty in less than a week.

"Are you nervous?" Craig asks, pulling up in front of her place.

We're in one of those condo parks, the kind where all the units, including the shrubbery that surrounds them, are cookie-cutter perfect. Mrs. Slather's is the one on the end. There's a rust-stained car parked out front and a few rolled-up newspapers on her welcome mat.

"Do you want me to come with you?" Craig asks.

I shake my head and climb out of the car, the necklace pressed in my palm. There are ten stairs up to her door. I climb them slowly, trying to calm myself down—to slow the pounding of my heart.

At the eighth stair, I pause and look back at Craig's car. He gives me a thumbs-up and I do the same back, grateful that he's here. And that I've come this far.

My fingers shaking slightly, I take a deep breath and continue to the door. Finally, I ring the bell. I can hear someone moving inside. The door opens a couple seconds later.

"Can I help you?" the woman asks.

She's older than I imagined, maybe in her late sixties, with silvery hair and a crooked mouth.

"Are you Jocelyn Slather?" I ask, hearing the quiver in my voice.

"Who are *you*?" Her tiny blue eyes narrow on me. The deep lines that surround them branch out like tree limbs.

"I think I have something of yours," I say, ignoring the question.

Her mouth tenses into a frown. "And I think you've got the wrong person."

She goes to shut the door, but I'm able to stop it by

jamming my foot into the doorway. I dangle the necklace in front of her eyes.

"Where did you get that?" She looks past me, toward the street, to see if I'm alone.

"Travis wanted you to have this."

"Who are you?" she repeats.

"I'm a friend of your son's."

"Well, my son is dead." She goes to shut the door again, but my foot is still jammed in the way.

"Please," I say. "I mean, I know it sounds crazy, but hear me out. I have dreams about him."

She shakes her head and leaves me at the door, tells me she's going to go call the police.

"Just wait," I insist, flinging the door wide.

Travis's mother picks up the phone and clicks it on.

And so I just spill it, blurting out every detail that Travis told me—about Mother's Day and the soggy French toast, how he gave her wildflowers, and how the necklace was ripped from her neck. "It was thrown across the bathroom," I tell her. "You looked for it everywhere, but couldn't find it. It was in the radiator."

Mrs. Slather stops dialing and drops the phone. Her hand trembles over her mouth.

"He wants you to know that he doesn't blame you for his death," I continue.

"How do you know all this?" she asks, coming toward me again.

"I dream about him," I repeat, holding the necklace out to her.

She takes it and tries to say something. Her mouth moves to form words, but nothing comes out.

"I know it doesn't make sense," I say, "but maybe it doesn't need to. Maybe the only thing that matters right now is that you stop living a life of guilt."

And maybe I'll do the same.

# Twelve

IT'S SATURDAY AFTERNOON, a full three weeks since my visit to Mrs. Slather.

And a full three weeks since I've seen Travis.

I'm sitting in Stanley's Coffee Shop with Craig and Raina, a large cup of regular positioned on the table in front of me, since, oddly enough, Stanley's bland-o blend is actually starting to grow on me.

"So, how are you holding up?" Craig asks.

I shrug, trying my best to stay optimistic. The truth is, aside from Travis's absence from my dreams, my life here *has* gotten more palatable—not unlike Stanley's java.

It's weird, but moving halfway across the country—far from all-things-Emma—has brought her closer. Just yesterday, when I was whipping up a batch of butterscotch pudding in the kitchen, I accidentally said Emma's name in front of my parents—since Emma and I used to barter over who would lick the spoon, the bowl, *and* the stray droplets of spilled batter—and neither of them snapped at me. They just sort of exchanged a look and, though I wouldn't stake my life on it, I'm pretty sure I saw a tiny smile wiggle across my mother's lips.

For her—and them—that's huge.

Then, about two and half weeks ago, I opened my closet to look at the skates, to really see them for the first time in five years—white with red stripes running down the sides, glittery pink laces, and a giant scratch on the front from when I wiped out doing a spin.

I took them out and left them by my desk, so I'd be forced to look at them all the time. After a couple days, the anxiety wore off and they became just skates. Nothing more. And so I ended up donating them to Goodwill, opting to remember my sister by thinking about all our butterscotch concoctions and the times we made blanket forts under the dining room table.

"You're looking a whole lot better," Raina says, repositioning one of the many barrettes that adorn her hair. "I mean, I was seriously considering staging a Clinique intervention for you."

"Well, thanks," I say, glancing at my reflection in the wall mirror behind her. Having finally gotten caught up on sleep, I'm no longer a walking zombie. Gone are the veins of redness that ran through my otherwise bright green eyes. So long, tired and pasty complexion; my skin seems, dare I say, glowing compared to just a month ago. And so does my hair—no longer the drab auburn tresses that hung down the sides of my face. It now looks down-right tousled.

"So, is it safe to assume your house is a ghost-free zone now?" Craig smiles, exposing the oh-so-adorable gap between his two front teeth.

"Well, I wouldn't go that far," I say, looking down at my wrist, where the bruise has finally healed. "I mean, sometimes, when I least expect it, I get a hint of him—a vibe, a feeling, a whiff of his spicy scent."

Like the other day when I was waking up, I could have sworn I felt someone clasp my hand. A few days before that, when I was getting dressed, I thought I spotted a hockey stick propped up against the wall, but, when I looked back, it was gone.

"So, he's still around," Craig says, trying to be clear.

"In some way, I guess, he always will be."

"That's totally hot." Raina grabs a sugar packet and attempts to fan herself down with it. "Any chance he has an available dead friend?"

I let out a laugh, wondering if Travis is watching over me right now, if he's happy where he is.

And if his heart aches, too.

"You should totally go on one of those ghost-hunter shows," she says. "You know . . . the kind where the psychics help solve crimes and stuff."

"I'm hardly psychic."

"Well, what else do you call it? Last I heard, it wasn't exactly mainstream to communicate with the dead—much less make out with them. How was that, by the way?"

I smile wide, just thinking about it. About him. Our last kiss in front of the lake, our fingers entwined, and our lips melted together.

"That good, huh?" Raina asks, winking at me. "I need to get me some ghost—fast."

"Right," Craig says, "because nobody with a pulse would possibly date you."

While they continue to bicker, I lean back in my seat, noticing the sudden warmth in my palm.

And the smell of spiced apples all around me.

# Stupid Perfect World

## SCOTT WESTERFELD

# One

*L*IKE MOST DAYS, I was barely on time for Scarcity class.

It wasn't a real course with grades and everything, so only the most pathetic meekers worked hard at it. The rest of us just showed up and tried not to fall asleep. Nobody wanted to *fail*, of course, because that meant repeating: another long semester of watching all those olden-day people starving and being diseased. At least regular History has battles; Scarcity was just depressing.

So when I walked in and saw what Mr. Solomon had written on the antique chalkboard, I groaned out loud.

FINAL PROJECT PROPOSALS DUE TODAY.

"Forget something, Kieran?" That was Maria Borsotti from the desk next to mine, her old-timey paper notebook out and ready to be scribbled in.

"This is *not* fair," I said, dropping into my seat. Assignments were supposed to appear in headspace automatically. But one of the rules of the Scarcity classroom was that all the decent tech was switched off. Just like our miserable, diseased ancestors, we had to rely on our own brains, or, like Maria Borsotti, scratch glyphs on to dead wood pulp.

Learn to write by hand? For a pass/fail class? What a meeker.

I'd *meant* to put a reminder up for myself. The projects were first-come, first-scourge (Scarcity humor = hilarious), so most people had shot right into headspace the moment class had ended on Friday, racing to look up the easiest diseases before anyone else claimed them.

We were supposed to "embody" some form of ancient lameness, spending the next two weeks being blind or whatever. This was supposed to teach us what things were really like in the old days, as if sitting through an hour of Scarcity every day wasn't depressing enough.

But I'd been distracted by Barefoot Tillman, who'd come up after class wanting help on an Antarctic camping trip. It's hard to say no to Barefoot—who's about two meters tall and the most beautiful girl in school. After talking tempsuits and penguins with her, I'd teleported straight to my climbing elective in the Alps. That started a busy weekend without pestilence or war or want: shopping with Mom on the moon, buckling down in headspace to work on my old-speak (my acting class was doing *Hamlet*), and spending all Sunday building my South Pole habitat for Advanced Engineering. The only time Scarcity had reared its diseased head was when my buddy Sho and I were simming some battle and I was like, "Whoa, people died a lot back then!" But then this airplane was bombing me, so I forgot again.

So here it was Monday, too late to do any research. As class officially began, headspace faded—my schedule, zero-g league scores, even the time of day, all gone. The world took on that weird, flat Scarcity look: one layer of vision, nothing to see but Maria Borsotti's self-satisfied smile.

"Poor Kieran," she said.

"Help me," I whispered.

She looked away. "Well, I *might* have had a couple of leftover ideas . . ."

Mr. Solomon started by clearing his throat. He said that was how people got your attention in the old days, because they were always ill.

"Well, people, I hope you're ready for a life-changing experience."

Low-level groans rumbled through the classroom.

Solomon raised his hands to silence us. "Perspective is the key to the next two weeks. This project shouldn't dismay you. In fact, the better you understand how things used to be, the happier you'll be about your lives now."

And that was the real point of Scarcity class: making us all into appreciative little meekers who never complained—even about really annoying things like, say, Scarcity class.

Maria shifted closer and murmured, "Oh, too bad. I can't seem to find my notes. But Mr. Solomon said he had a few extra ideas."

I swallowed. Our teacher had threatened a serious nightmare project for anyone who didn't come up with their own. Bubonic plague, maybe. Or athlete's foot, which sounded like a good thing to have, but wasn't. I felt like one of those nerdy kids who can't find a buddy in gym class and has to run laps instead of playing zero-g.

"Who wants to go first?" Mr. Solomon asked.

Hands shot up, everyone eager to lock in their projects. I sat there frozen, my unassisted brain spinning hopelessly. Solomon called on Barefoot Tillman first.

"Can I do the common cold?" she asked.

I glared at her. It was Barefoot's fault I'd forgotten this assignment, and she was picking *cold*? After all the famines and pandemics we'd watched this semester? Even nowadays people got cold *sometimes*. Like down at the Pole, my tempsuit was always icy when I first put it on in the morning. Distinctly unpleasant. And "common cold" sounded a lot lamer than South Pole cold.

A smile was spreading across Mr. Solomon's face.

"Are you sure you want to attempt something so . . . disagreeable?"

That seemed to take Barefoot by surprise, and I saw from Maria's grin that she'd already investigated this "common cold," and if a meeker like Maria wanted no part of it, Barefoot was in big trouble.

"I can handle it," she said, bluffing. Her thumbs were twitching with unconscious headspace gestures, trying to check closer. Knowing Barefoot, she hadn't gotten past the name. It's that kind of lazy work that Scarcity is supposed to teach you not to rely on, because people used to die from being lazy.

Of course, Barefoot was still way ahead of me.

"Well then," Mr. Solomon said, "the common cold is all yours, Miss Tillman. Enjoy."

More hands shot up.

Solomon's gaze took a random walk around the classroom. This whole raising-your-hand thing was another of the tech-stepdowns that made Scarcity so frustrating. You had to wait your turn instead of arguing on multiple audio levels or texting on to one big thread. No wonder they were always fighting back then—discussing anything complicated with a single audio level was like trying to suck tar through a straw.

Lao Wrigley had her hand up higher than anyone.

"I'd like to do physical transport. No teleporting at all." She flicked her hair. "My dad flies me to school anyway."

"What an ambitious bunch you are," Solomon said, the sadistic glee on his face making my stomach flip. "But what about your classes on other continents?"

Lao smugly shuffled the paper in her hands. She wasn't a Maria Borsotti–level meeker, but she always squirted her notes from headspace on to wood-pulp before class.

"Well, my courses in Asia are all in headspace this semester, so I don't have to teleport. My skin-diving elective is down in the Bahamas, but there's this cargo ferry that runs twice a day, and it has some old passenger seats."

Mr. Solomon nodded. "Excellent research, Lao, but I think you'll find that boats are surprisingly slow. Did you know how long it takes?"

Lao nodded solemnly. "Two whole hours, Mr. S. But I can manage it if our ancestors could."

"And what about your social life, Miss Wrigley? This means no parties on Luna for two weeks."

Still wearing her serious face, Lao folded her hands. "Well, Scarcity doesn't mean much unless you have to give something up."

I rolled my eyes—as if Lao Wrigley had a planet-hopping social life. Even Maria raised an eyebrow, like she'd just sent me a headspace message. (That was the one cool thing about Scarcity: it made you realize how much you could communicate using just your face.) We managed not to giggle out loud.

Mr. Solomon nodded and started looking for his next victim.

Now my brain was really racing. It hadn't occurred to me that you could give up teleporting. I'd been focused on the classics: diseases or starvation or having a limb paralyzed. Maybe a tech-stepdown was safer than some bacteria running rampant in my body.

I tried to remember all the olden-day hassles. No teleporting (taken). No headspace (yeah, right). No tempsuits (so I'd freeze to death down at the Pole?). No guaranteed credit level (and what would that mean— getting a job?). Every idea sounded nightmarish.

I guess that was the point of Scarcity: it sucked *inescapably*.

"How are those ideas coming, Kieran?" Maria whispered.

I gritted my teeth, having the sulky realization that my ancestors had expended lots of effort figuring out how not to suffer from hunger and lion attacks and random germs growing inside them. Much appreciated, ancient forebears, but why should *I* have to run that gauntlet again?

Though the thought of lions *was* kind of cool. I wondered if I could do predation, and have a fabricator build some big beast to chase me every now and then. But it would probably annoy my acting teacher, getting jumped by cave bears while rehearsing Shakespeare.

Solomon went through my classmates one by one, the noose tightening as hands went down.

My buddy Sho took hunger, saying he thought it would be funny to get skinny. His bioframe wouldn't let him die, after all, and people used to fast for two weeks all the time. Solomon said okay, but made him promise to drink lots of water.

Judy Watson chose illiteracy, which meant she could only use icons and verbal commands in headspace. This was an excellent dodge, given how many people didn't bother reading anymore. I tried to think of some variation on the idea, but nothing worked—and I needed to be literate to learn my lines for *Hamlet*.

Most people took diseases: cancers or infections, even a few parasites. Dan Stratovaria took river blindness, so his eyes would get eaten away over the next two weeks. Solomon let him keep visuals in headspace to do homework with, and Dan had been planning on getting new eyes anyway, so score another one for easy.

The only diseases I could remember were the ones with funny names, like whooping cough. But two weeks of whooping didn't sound like fun.

"You're cute when you're nervous," Maria whispered.

Mr. Solomon's gaze shifted our way. "Maria and Kieran, what have you two been discussing so furiously since class began?"

"Well, Kieran has an outstanding idea, Mr. Solomon," Maria said, and I suppressed the urge to kick her.

"No doubt, Maria," he said. "But let's hear yours first."

Maria just smiled. "I'd like to suspend my hormonal balancers."

Solomon nodded slowly—apparently these words made sense to him. "A little risky at sixteen years of age, don't you think?"

"It'll be fun, finding out how it was to be a teenager back then." She shrugged. "It always sounds really intense when you read about it."

"Indeed it does. Let the hormones run free, then. And what about *your* outstanding idea, Kieran?"

I ignored Maria's amused expression. "Well, I was thinking about trying something . . . different."

"Wonderful. And what would that be?"

What indeed? *What?* I tried to think of something that would help me with mountain climbing, like a fear of heights. Or motivate my Antarctic skills, like the possibility of frostbite. Or help me understand *Hamlet* better, because those Elizabethan times had been all about the heavy-duty scarcity . . .

And with that thought, William Shakespeare came to my rescue.

"Sleep," I said.

"Ah." Mr. Solomon steepled his fingers, looking

pleased. "Very original."

"Of course, I don't mean *tons* of sleep," I added quickly. "But some every single night, like they used to. Um, right?"

"Well, I don't suppose I'll make you put in eight hours," he said. "As long as you get down to REM."

I nodded, pretending I had some idea what "REM" was, while I was thinking, *Eight hours a night?* How did olden-day people get anything done? Most months I skipped my one hour of brainsmoothing.

A hint of panic must have crept onto my face, because Solomon said, "I believe that some ancients slept as little as three or four hours a night. Perhaps you can do some *research* on the matter."

I smiled sheepishly, just thankful that I'd escaped bubonic plague.

# Two

I T's NOT LIKE KIERAN Black was cute or anything.

His outdoorsy mania had a certain charm, the way he teleported to classes straight from Antarctica, icicles clinging to his hair, lips freshly chapped by freezing winds. And he'd been attractively clueless that day, not realizing that hanging out at the South Pole was pretty much a Scarcity project already. I mean, who went outside in the cold these days?

So when class ended, I decided to take pity on him.

"Need some help?" I offered. "In my Bio unit, we have this hamster who sleeps."

Kieran looked at me like he thought I was teasing him again, but then gave a tiny nod. Our projects were supposed to start right away, and he probably didn't know the first thing about getting to sleep.

Sho Walters strolled past us and whacked Kieran's shoulder. "Sweet project, bud. Lying there doing nothing."

"Pretty good one, huh?" Kieran said, punching back. "But it isn't like forgetting to eat is so hard."

"Hey, I *enjoy* eating!" Sho called, then gave me a funny look as he slipped out into the hall.

I rolled my eyes, wondering if this outreach program was pointless. Sho lived by the rules that schoolwork was stupid, understanding was overrated, and effort was for meekers. If Kieran was the same way, I didn't have time for posturing.

But then he muttered, "And I enjoy not lying around. I've got a snow habitat to build."

I smiled. *A snow habitat?* Maybe this boy was worth my effort.

As the last few students slipped out of the classroom, a bemused look settled on Kieran's face. "So is that all you do when you sleep? Lie there doing nothing?"

"That's what Mikey the hamster does," I said. "He breathes, but that's about it."

"Yeah, but he's a *hamster*. Didn't people back then get really bored?"

"You can't be bored when you're unconscious, silly."

"Oh, right, unconscious. So like when you get major surgery."

"No, it's like . . ." I shook my head. "Kieran, you didn't

do *any* research on this, did you?"

"Not really. I was busy all weekend."

"How did you even manage to come up with sleep?"

"Well, it's in this play we're doing. This psycho prince guy is thinking about suicide, and saying how death might not be so bad, because he figures it's like sleep." He shrugged. "So I figured it couldn't totally suck."

"You've read *Hamlet*?" I said, perplexed. Could Kieran Black possess hidden depths? Sure, he'd just called the greatest character in literature "this psycho prince guy," but still.

"Yeah, I can read," he said. "Didn't mean to shock you. Maybe you thought I ran around in a little wheel all day?"

"Oh, that would be *so* cute."

He rolled his eyes at me, then glanced into headspace and sighed. "We should get going. For the next two weeks, I'm wasting three hours a day."

I took Kieran straight to my Bio classroom, which had both a hamster *and* a customizing engine for bioframes. I already had the program that would shut down my hormone balancers—those little widgets that keep us calm and collected and boring all the time.

*Teen angst, here I come.*

A few other people from Scarcity were already there, needing the engine to switch off immune defenses and organ repair. The machine's AI was taking forever, checking permission slips and running simulations to make sure no one altered their bioframe in a lethal or illegal way. And, of course, Barefoot Tillman had managed to be first in line.

Kieran wandered over to Mikey's habitat and looked down at his little quivering form. "Is he asleep right now?"

I stuck a finger through the confining field, and Mikey sniffed it.

"Nope. Just resting. See how his little eyes are open?"

Kieran reached through gingerly and stroked the hamster's fur. Mikey stirred, then settled back down.

"Hey, his eyes just closed! So he's asleep now?"

I sighed. "I think it takes longer than two seconds, Kieran. In old stories, sometimes people can't get to sleep at all, like if they're worked up about emotional stuff. It's called 'tossing and turning.'"

He looked up at me. "How do you know all this stuff, anyway?"

"Just from reading historicals, I guess. It's awesome how their emotions worked back then. They'd have these little bouts of temporary insanity all the time." I watched his finger run down Mikey's back. "Just meeting a cute guy or girl could make them go crazy."

"That still happens," he said. "I forgot about this project just because Barefoot Tillman talked to me."

"That's *not* what I'm talking about," I snapped. "Barefoot's just distracting, not epic at all. Back then, it was screaming fights and weeping for hours. Pulling your hair out. Tossing and turning all night."

He laughed. "Sounds like a pain."

"Don't you pay *any* attention in Scarcity? Pain's a good thing. That's why we never cured it."

"Oh, right. Nature's way of saying, 'Get your hand out of the fire, doofus!'" As he spoke, Kieran lifted his fingers gently from the confinement field.

Mikey looked like he might actually be asleep now. I guess Kieran had pretty decent hamster-wrangling skills. I let myself smile, my annoyance on the Barefoot Tillman issue settling.

"Is that why you want to do that hormone thing?" Kieran asked. "To go crazy?"

"Well . . . not *totally* crazy. But don't you ever wonder what it would be like to feel how they did back then? Especially people our age. It was more extreme, more . . . dramatic. I mean, why do you go down to the South Pole and put up with that freezing cold? Because it's intense, right?"

Kieran was staring down at the dozing hamster. "Yeah. But cold doesn't make me lose my mind."

"Still, it's something no one else feels. Not these days."

"I guess." He shrugged and smiled. "Just don't get too

crazy and drown yourself, Maria. Or write any poetry."

I had to laugh. "Don't worry, I'll try not to go completely Ophelia. As long as I don't meet any psycho prince guys in the next two weeks."

The line for the customizing engine was winding down. People headed out for the rest of their afternoon classes, a few laughing nervously. Dan Stratovaria was rubbing his eyes, as if trying to feel the long-extinct worms growing inside them.

I was a little anxious myself, now that my moment of hormonal imbalance was actually at hand. The next two weeks would probably be embarrassing. Though my bioframe wouldn't let me kill myself, there *was* a definite danger of poetry. . . .

"Come on, let's do some research." I flicked headspace up to full, the Bio room and Mikey's habitat fading in front of my eyes. "If we don't figure out how sleep works, you're going to be tossing and turning all night."

# Three

THE FIRST PROBLEM WAS finding the right furniture.

When I got home, I asked Dad if I could synthesize a bed for my room. He immediately put on his serious face and sat me down.

"Sixteen is too young to have a bed in your room, Kieran. Remember when we talked about this, how a little bioframe tweak can make those feelings less . . . persistent?"

I groaned. "This isn't about that, Dad!"

"Who was that girl you were obsessed with last summer? Chrissy?"

"Chris*tine*," I said. "And this has nothing to do with girls. It's for a school project."

He laughed too hard in a really embarrassing way,

actually slapping his thigh. "Nice try, buddy."

"No, really. It's for Scarcity!" I started to explain my project, but as usual Dad's brain switched off. There hadn't been any Scarcity classes back in his day, and he never understood how I could get worked up over an ungraded course.

By the time my explanation sputtered out, his serious face was back. "So, Kieran. Is there anyone special you want to tell me about?"

I groaned again. This was useless. At least Mom wasn't around, which would have been twice as embarrassing. "Just forget I brought it up."

"Are you sure, son? You know I'm here if you need me."

I rolled my eyes and headed to my room.

Around midnight I gave it my best shot.

A pile of parkas wasn't a terrible bed. It was a lot more comfortable than the furniture I'd been making out of snow. I sank into the thermal fibers, closing my eyes and trying to feel for any changes inside me.

It had been about eight hours since Maria had switched off the metabolic nanos that kept my body humming twenty-four hours a day. For the next two weeks, my cells were going to divide their time the old-fashioned way: breaking down complex molecules while I was awake, and building up new ones while I slept. Not as efficient as doing both at once, but nothing I had to consciously control. Even Mikey the hamster could do it.

I darkened the room to make it like outside at night, then I lay there with my eyes closed, waiting for some kind of change.

According to headspace, there were five stages of sleep. Stage 1 was no big deal, like that feeling right after a brainsmoothing session, when everything's fuzzy for a few minutes. Stage 2 was exactly how sleep looks in old movies: lying around unconscious, like after surgery or getting hit on the head. Basically your average waste of time, except you couldn't be bored, which was a bonus.

I wasn't looking forward to Stage 3, which featured these weird interruptions like sleepwalking, sleep-*talking*, night terrors, and something called "bedwetting." (Don't ask.) Luckily, that part usually passed quickly, and then it was on to Stages 4 and 5, but it wasn't like I'd researched every detail yet. I was just hoping to get to Stage 1 tonight.

So I waited some more.

And waited . . .

I won't say that *nothing* happened. I thought about lots of stuff: my lines for *Hamlet*, Dad's lameness, Barefoot Tillman in a swimsuit, Mikey the hamster, the way Maria Borsotti might be cute if she wasn't such a meeker. But it wasn't exactly sleep. I had so many thoughts, it was the opposite of unconsciousness; I was suddenly conscious of every sound in my room, every worry in my head, and especially every itch and crick in my motionless body.

I wasn't supposed to move, but my muscles kept demanding random adjustments. By the end of the first hour, I was tangled in the parkas and ended up throwing half of them across my room. (Is that where "tossing and turning" came from?) I hadn't noticed any unconsciousness, but then I started wondering how you could even know you were unconscious, because you wouldn't be conscious to know anything at all, which started my head spinning with thoughts and thoughts and more thoughts.

Finally, I sat up, not caring if I failed Scarcity, anything to escape the crushing, sweaty boredom of not sleeping.

And lo and behold, my three hours were almost up.

But it hadn't *seemed* that long. Was that because I'd never been still that long before, so I had nothing to compare it to? Or had there been a little bit of missing time in all that tossing and turning—a tiny sliver of sleep?

If so, that was kind of cool—almost like some lame form of time travel. My head felt a little fuzzy, but I knew a quick shot of Antarctic wind would clear that up. I slipped on a tempsuit and headed for the teleporter, for the first time thinking that this project might not totally suck.

It wasn't until later that day that I really started to feel weird.

# *Four*

KIERAN BLACK LOOKED LIKE crap. Crap covered with icicles.

"Are you okay?"

A shiver went through him. "Yeah, fine, Maria. I was just down at Amundsen-Scott Station. That's at the South Pole."

"Um, Kieran? No kidding." I reached across the space between our desks and pulled away a tiny icicle clinging to his hair. It gave my fingertips a cold little kiss, then melted in my palm.

"This weird thing happened," he said. "I was smoothing down the outside of my habitat with a blowtorch, and I started feeling funny. So I sat down in the snow, which you're not supposed to do in winter, really. I was sitting there and sort of lost track of time . . . until my bioframe gave me a frostbite warning."

My jaw dropped. "You mean you *fell asleep*? Already?"

He nodded, and I sighed. Even Kieran Black was ahead of me. I hadn't felt anything yet, except maybe more than the usual annoyance at my mother, who'd *insisted* on criticizing every item of clothing I'd worn today. Like I'd never been in an all-black mood before.

"I'm not totally sure," Kieran said. A shiny sliver of tempsuit was sticking out from his shirt top, radiating warmth like he'd forgotten to turn it off. The icicles were melting fast. "I definitely didn't get much last night."

"But you got *some*? What was it like?"

"I don't know." He blinked. "I think when you're asleep you don't know it. So . . . it's not like anything."

I frowned. I'd been expecting this project to make Kieran Black more interesting. But apparently it was just making him kind of slow.

I started to check and see if that was normal, but no sooner had headspace appeared than it faded back into flat reality.

Scarcity was starting.

"So how was everyone's first day?" Mr. Solomon asked.

"I have to change my project, Mr. Solomon," Lao Wrigley began. "It isn't safe."

She'd spoken without raising her hand, which Mr. Solomon usually corrected. But today he calmly interlaced his fingers, like he'd been expecting a few complaints. "Not safe?"

"Not at all!" Lao gripped the sides of her desk. "I took the boat thing this morning, and the ocean was completely messed up!"

"Could you be referring to *waves*, Miss Wrigley?"

Barefoot Tillman, who always bragged about her stupid surfing trophies, stifled a laugh, and I grinned at Kieran. He didn't respond.

His expression was strangely peaceful, and he didn't stir as the last icicles melted from his hair, drops rolling down his neck and into his shirt. Watching it, I felt a matching trickle of sweat on my own back, hot instead of cold.

*That* was an interesting feeling.

"Yes, the ocean does have waves," Mr. Solomon was patiently explaining. "But ships are designed for waves. I'm sure it's perfectly safe out there."

Lao shook her head. "Oh, yeah? Well, if ships are so safe, why is there a word for them turning upside down?"

"Pardon me?"

"*Capsizing*, Mr. Solomon!" Lao said. "That's a special word just for ships turning upside down. I checked in headspace, and I couldn't find a single word for trains turning upside down! Or cars or hovercraft—just ships. Think about it!"

"Miss Wrigley, I doubt your cargo ship is in danger of capsizing."

"But it's awful!" Her head fell into her hands. "I also did the math wrong."

"The math?"

"Turns out it takes two hours *each way*!"

A smiled flickered on Solomon's face. "But of course, Miss Wrigley. Did you forget you had to come back?"

I raised an eyebrow. Those extra two hours would have gotten past me, too. It wasn't like it had ever taken me longer than five seconds to get anywhere in the world. Even Mars was only a three-minute teleport away.

Lao looked up from her hands, swallowing, and I noticed that her skin was paler than usual. "Four hours every day! And when I tried to get some reading done this morning, the waves made me feel really weird!"

"Ah . . ." Mr. Solomon nodded. "I believe you have something called *seasickness*. If you check headspace later, you'll probably find a few old bioframe patches for it. Your Scarcity project has no medical restrictions, after all." He chuckled. "But there's no cure for having to go both ways in a journey. I'm afraid you're stuck with that. How's everyone else?"

As more hands went up, I looked closer at Lao. Now that I'd noticed it, she definitely was a weird color. Hints of blue-green in her face, like the sea. Is that why they called it seasickness?

Barefoot raised her hand. "My common cold is going great. I like the way it makes my voice sound."

I frowned. Her voice *was* sort of lower, like a soft growl. Leave it to Barefoot to bag a project that made her even sexier.

At least Kieran wasn't staring at her today. His gaze was lost in the black depths of the chalkboard.

I raised my hand. "Mr. Solomon? I think something's wrong with Kieran."

At the sound of his name, Kieran snapped out of his catatonic state to glare at me. "No, I'm fine."

"Just checking." I smiled sweetly.

"I'm sure Kieran simply feels a little unusual," Mr. Solomon said. "I believe the technical term is 'sleepy.' But you're all going to feel a lot stranger as these projects go on. Today is only the beginning, so stop gnawing on your sleeve, Sho."

"My sleeve isn't food!"

"No, but it's annoying." Mr. Solomon sighed, looking at Lao Wrigley again. She had started making weird noises in the back of her throat, and her face was definitely the green of a shallow sea.

I looked down at my blank notebook, fingers curling around my pen.

*The green of a shallow sea,* I wrote. The words looked frail and fragile in my spindly hand. All that time spent learning to write, and I'd hardly taken any notes this semester.

Suddenly, I wanted to incise the white surface of the paper.

Lao made a distinct gagging noise.

"Hmm, perhaps we should end class early today," Mr. Solomon said. "On account of seasickness. You and I can head straight to the Biology Department, Lao. And everyone else, try to spend some of this unexpected hour of freedom thinking about your project. Take note of the changes within you."

I smiled at his words, writing, *The changes within me* . . .

I had lots of notes to take.

# Five

THIS PROJECT SUCKED.

On top of losing three hours a day, I was brain-dead the other twenty-one. All week I'd shuffled through my classes like a zombie in one of Sho's combat games. Suddenly all my lines for *Hamlet* were missing from my head. I tried to explain to Ms. Parker that it was all Mr. Solomon's fault, but she said that was no excuse because actors in the olden days had slept every single night.

Yeah . . . but they *knew how*!

So at midnight, there I was again, staring at my make-shift bed with the usual tangled emotions. On the one hand, looking at the crumpled parkas made me want to strangle Solomon with a fleece-lined sleeve. But at the same time, somehow, the pile looked lovely. There was nothing I wanted more than to lie down on it. Waves of dizziness were drifting over me.

Maybe tonight it would finally work.

I dropped on to the pile, my face landing in a collar of fake fur. The hairs ruffled softly against my lips as I breathed in and out. I told the room to darken, and silence began to settle around me. . . .

A communication chime sounded, breaking the spell.

"Yeah?" I sighed.

"It's me," Maria's voice said. "Can I come over?"

"Um, now's not good."

"Hey, you sound kind of . . . Oh, crap! I forgot what time it was. Were you sleeping?"

"Not yet," I murmured. "Well, maybe Stage One-ish."

"Oh, sorry," she whispered but didn't hang up. Her breathing floated invisibly in the air around me, soothing in the darkness.

It felt weird, together in silence like that, so I said, "I think it's going to go better tonight. Of course, I thought that last night, too."

"Hmm. Is your bed comfortable?"

"Well . . ." I didn't want to go into Dad's whole bed issue with Maria. "I haven't gotten that sorted out yet. I'm just sleeping on a pile of parkas."

"No bed?" Her giggle traveled through the room. "I hope you have pajamas on at least."

"Pa-whatses?"

She laughed again. "You're not supposed to wear regular clothes to bed, silly. Olden-day people had these special sleeping clothes. They had sleepy pictures on them. No wonder it's not working."

"I don't think that's the problem," I mumbled.

"But I don't think everyone had pajamas. Some people pulled these sheet things over them and were naked underneath."

"Now that makes sense." I yanked my shirt off over my head. It *was* more comfortable this way, so I kicked off my shoes and squirmed out of my pants. "Yeah, this is much better."

"Did you just—" she started, but her breath caught.

"Mm-hmm. Thanks for the suggestion." I settled into the pile, the fleece and thermal fibers soft against my skin. "It feels weird here in the dark. Like I'm turning weightless."

"Weightless in the dark," she repeated slowly.

The void behind my eyelids had grown deeper, a heaviness descending on me, finally squeezing out the rapid fire of my thoughts. "Yeah, it's weird. Like the world's being erased."

"The world erased . . ."

"What are you doing?"

"Oh, I was just copying some stuff down," she said. "I'm sort of . . . keeping a journal of my project."

"Solomon will love that," I murmured.

"It's not for *him*. It's only for me. . . . Want to hear some?"

I must have grunted, because Maria started reading to me. It was more random than any diary, more like phrases snatched from conversations, words repeating and tangling without ever making meaning. Soothingly senseless, like drifting clouds of language.

But whatever it was she'd written, the sound of her voice worked wonders. An enchantment fell across me, the darkness carried me swiftly toward Stage 2, the world finally evaporating. No doubt I passed through 3 and into 4 in pretty quick succession.

And later that night, very definitely, I fell all the way down to Stage 5 . . . where I dreamed.

# Six

FTER HE FELL ASLEEP, I listened to him breathe for a long time.

My own skin felt wrong, hypersensitive to my clinging clothes, to every shift of air. While we'd been talking, I'd dimmed the lights to match my mental image of Kieran's room, and now the darkness seemed tangible around me, a physical thing, pressing against my hungry skin.

The white pages of my notebook glowed in my hands, still demanding attention. It was as if the paper had grown thirstier for words as I read from it.

Especially when I read aloud to a naked, almost sleeping boy.

I could picture him there in his pile of puffy coats, vulnerable and perfectly still. It maddened me that he was so far away, out of reach of my aching skin. But there was also something intense in disembodiment, as if distance amplified our connection.

My hormones were definitely roiling now, flexing their muscles. But being out of balance wasn't what I'd expected; there were no sudden fits of madness, no breathtaking epiphanies. It was almost subtle—like the flickers of desire that rose and fell with the sound of Kieran's breathing.

I started scribbling again, trying to spill the slow pressure inside me on to paper. As words poured out, a rumble gradually built up around me. It took ages to realize that the sound wasn't in my head—it was coming from the window. Rain drummed against it, blurring the lights of the other high-rises.

I jumped up and put my hand against the glass, felt the cold and condensation, and suddenly I wanted to be outside—*in the rain*. That was what lovelorn heroines always did in the old stories: they ran outside and screamed their frustrations away! (And then they got sick and almost died, but I could skip that part.)

I stared out at the downpour, letting out a groan . . .

Mom's apartment wasn't like the old-fashioned house we'd lived in when Dad was alive. The high-rises didn't have doors to the outside; you came and went through the teleporter. The gardens and lawns around us were just for looking at, the mountains in the distance all national parkland, forbidden and protected.

Stupid perfect world.

My fingernails skated the edges of the window, but there were no buttons to press, no latch or lock. All I wanted was to feel the rain on my hands! But windows that opened were too dangerous.

The boiling under my skin was much worse now; my hormones had sniffed freedom. My blood felt trapped inside me. And on top of it all, I heard Kieran Black breathing again—the voice call still connected.

It was like he was inside me, his slow rhythm stuck in my head, something invisible and ancient connecting us.

I sat down on the floor with my notebook, grabbed for the pen, and cut into the paper with quick strokes.

> *In this tower with no doors,*
> *My skin hunger pulses,*
> *Like his breathing in my ears,*
> *So near and yet . . .*

"Oh, crap," I cried, staring at the staggered lines of handwriting. I hadn't been keeping a journal . . . I'd been writing *poetry*.

I had to get out of here, out into the rain and oxygen. I grabbed my jacket again and ran toward the teleporter, checking in headspace for somewhere—*anywhere*—

that it was raining. Climate Watch informed me that it was pouring in Paris, drizzling in Delhi, and that a monsoon was skirting Madras—all five seconds away.

But I hesitated inside the teleporter; it seemed wrong to go ten thousand kilometers. I wanted that rain *right there*, on the other side of my window.

Then I saw the fire evacuation stickers on the wall— maps and procedures for when teleportation failed— and smiled.

"Sky deck," I told the teleporter, not wanting to climb thirty flights of emergency stairs.

The huge room twinkled into view. It was empty, of course. Nothing to see tonight through the floor-to-ceiling windows, streaks of rain concealing the dark mountains in the distance. The stars in the sky were washed away, even the moon a blur . . .

*The moon a blur?* Argh. I was *thinking* in poetry now!

I looked around for the soft red pulse of the fire exit, pulling the jacket across my shoulders as I ran. The storm was deafening up here, the rain driven by high-altitude winds.

EVACUATION ONLY, the door warned, less than poetic.

I placed my palm flat against its cold metal surface,

bit my bottom lip, having a last moment of hesitation—afraid to break the rules.

"*Meeker,*" I hissed at myself. That's what Kieran Black thought of me, with my Scarcity-era notebook and pen, scribbling to impress Mr. Solomon.

Well, this was the door out of my stupid perfect world, a door for calamities and conflagrations, and for when things were *on fire* . . .

I shoved it hard, and a shrieking filled my ears. A dingy flight of stairs led upward, harsh lights flickering to life overhead. A canned voice broke into the alarm, asking the nature of the emergency, but I ignored it and dashed toward the roof. Two flights up was another door, plastered with stickers warning of high winds and low temperatures, of edges without safety rails, of unfiltered, cancer-causing sunlight—all the uncontrollable dangers of *outside.*

I pushed the door cautiously, but the wind reached in and yanked it open with the crash of metal. The rain tore inside, streaming across me. I was frozen for a terrified moment; the rushing blackness seemed too vast and powerful. But that calm, infuriating voice kept asking where the fire was, driving me outside.

The wind grew stronger with every step I took. A few meters from the door, my jacket was stripped from my shoulders, disappearing into the darkness. Half-frozen drops streaked out of the dark sky, battering my face and bare arms, feeding my hungry skin.

I opened up my hands to feel the rain drum against my palms, and opened my mouth to drink the cold water, laughing and wishing that Kieran Black was there beside me.

Two minutes later, security arrived and took me home.

# Seven

"MORE *DRAMA*, PEOPLE!" Ms. Parker cried.

Everyone just stared at her, swords drooping. We'd been practicing this scene for hours, trying to get the blocking right. Most of this was William Shakespeare's fault; it's pretty hard to switch two swords in the middle of a fight *by accident*. Come on.

The so-called army waiting off-stage was growing restless. Every time they got ready to march in with a warlike volley, Ms. Parker cut in, complaining about the lack of drama. Too bad nobody had taken death-by-poisoning for their Scarcity project—they could have showed us how. . . .

"Okay, take a break," she finally said in disgust.

Everyone headed to the green room or over to the teleporters, but I sheathed my sword and slid off the edge of the stage, climbing up through the empty seats. The quiet out here was a relief from forgotten lines, implausible blocking, and Ms. Parker's demands for *drama*.

I sat down in the last row, a few seats in from the aisle, and tipped my head back. My eyes closed automatically, and I felt the soothing darkness close around me.

Sleeping, it turned out, was awesome. I was clocking six hours a night now, plus naps. The lost time was killing my grades, but I loved slipping away into oblivion and consummation.

And the psycho prince guy had been wrong to worry: Stage 5 sleep wasn't a rub at all. It had all the drama our production was missing, and I was devoutly addicted to it.

Since that first real sleep, Maria had been reading to me every night. It was an actual olden-day tradition called "bedtime stories," according to Maria. And even though her journal was just random sentences, she did spin stories in my head. The sound of her voice made dreams happen.

It felt like talking in Shakespeare's old-speak, using "dreaming" to mean Stage 5. That old definition had disappeared along with sleep itself. Nowadays people only "dreamed" of bigger houses or getting famous.

But I kept wondering how close the two meanings were. Did I really *want* everything I saw in REM sleep? Should I risk making real what I did there, or should I keep it safely hidden in my dreams?

"Kieran," came a whisper from right beside me.

I jumped, my eyes flying open.

"You okay?" Maria asked softly.

"Oh, sorry." I blinked, for a moment wondering if this was real or not. "I was just napping."

"Awesome." Her smile glimmered in the stage lights. "How's the Bard going?"

"Not dramatic enough for Ms. Parker." I let out a sigh. "I'm not sure what would be, except maybe a hurricane blowing off the roof."

"Ooh . . ." she breathed softly. "A hurricane would be fun."

I smiled. She'd told me about her trip to the roof, her wild dancing and her skin hunger—all of it had wormed its way into my dreams.

She leaned in close, her breath in my ear. "I have a question for you."

"We don't have to whisper," I said. "We're on break."

"But I like whispering. It makes things more . . . dramatic."

A shiver went through me.

"Speaking of which." Maria turned back to the empty stage, where the lights were shifting between palettes, sword-fight red to soliloquy blue. "Tonight when I read to you . . . maybe it would be better in person. I mean, more dramatic, from right beside your bed."

I knew what she was asking, of course. I'd been asking it myself a moment before. But I wasn't sure how you went from dreams to reality without the magic leaking out—or becoming too wild and powerful.

Truth was, I was kind of scared of Maria these days.

Her stare had grown more intense every day of the project. Here in the darkness of the auditorium she looked ready for one of her prized bouts of insanity. Especially if I said the wrong thing.

"Maria, it's awesome when you read to me. I love your voice, I don't think I could go to sleep without it. But I think that . . ."

"That you only like my *voice*?" she asked.

"No!" My dreams had gone way beyond Maria's voice. Images flashed in my mind's eye, as vivid as memories of real events. But how could I say that out loud? "It's just that . . . dreaming can be weird."

Her breath caught in the dark. "You started *dreaming*? Since when?"

"Since the first time you read to me," I said.

"And you didn't *tell* me?"

"Well, it's kind of embarrassing."

She leaned closer, her mad eyes flashing. "*What's* embarrassing?"

I squirmed in the hard wooden chair, my brain rejecting this collision between dream life and reality. I thought of how Stage 5 sleep makes your eyelids twitch, your hands quiver, and how I woke up every morning with drool on my face. Maybe that was something she'd understand?

Here in the second week, all the projects were getting weird. Barefoot Tillman's common cold had turned freakish—her eyes were all puffy and red. Strange colors of goo ran out of her nose, and she had to carry around paper towels to collect it. Even Dan Stratovaria—his eyes were milky white and his skin riddled with white veins—steered clear of her. He'd gone blind over the weekend, but had learned to avoid the honking noises Barefoot made.

"Okay, I'll tell you. But it's weird."

"Weird how?"

I swallowed. Did I really want to tell Maria about my drool? "Well, you know how Barefoot—"

"Barefoot Tillman!" she hissed. "You're dreaming of *her*!"

"No! I was just—"

"Just *using* me!" she shrieked. "It's *my* voice you go to sleep to every night!" A scream spilled from her lips and through the auditorium. "What am I, some kind of Cyrano de Bergerac for bimbos?"

"No! Um . . . Cyrano who?"

"You illiterate, pathetic excuse for a rogue! I can't *believe* you!"

She leaped from her seat and stormed away up the aisle.

"Maria, wait!" I called. "That's not what I—"

"Goodbye, Kieran . . . and have a good *night*!" she screamed from the exit.

The door slammed behind her, a vast boom echoing through the silent auditorium. As I slumped back into my seat, I realized that stage and audience had been reversed: the assembled cast and crew were staring at me, eyes wide and jaws dropped open.

I leaned my head back, praying that this, too, was a dream.

The silence lingered for a moment, and then a single pair of hands began to clap out a slow beat. It was Ms. Parker perched on the edge of the stage, applauding with a broad smile on her face.

"Take notes, people," she declared. "Because *that* was drama!"

# Eight

MIDNIGHT WAS ALMOST HERE, and Kieran still hadn't called.

The bathwater burbled just beneath my nose, its warmth enveloping me, keeping my skin hunger barely in check. I closed my eyes and sank down until its rumble filled my ears, shutting out the deafening silence.

I still couldn't believe what he'd done, stealing *my* poetry to dream about Barefoot. And added to his theft was cowardice, hiding the betrayal inside his own subconscious. And he still hadn't called.

Maybe the rest was silence between us.

I stayed under the water, holding my breath, imagining Kieran's face when my tragic death by drowning was announced. After my explosion in the auditorium, everyone would realize he'd killed me with his dirty little dreams. I visualized the whole world knowing, my poems found and posthumously broadcast throughout headspace, along with cruel comparisons of my angelic death mask with Barefoot Tillman's puffy, snot-filled face.

As the fantasy progressed, the oxygen in my lungs ran out, my brain growing fuzzy, my heart thudding harder and harder inside my chest . . .

. . . until my bioframe sent me bursting up into the air, sputtering for breath.

"I wasn't *really* going to!" I muttered between gasps for air. Stupid perfect world.

I sank back down to shoulder height in the water, the memory of my auditorium outburst twisting in my stomach. All those times I'd imagined going crazy with olden-day emotions, the madness had taken place on a Scottish moor, a high balcony, or in a richly appointed boudoir—never in front of an *audience.*

Apparently, hormones went hand in hand with humiliation.

I tried to remember what had happened in the fight, exactly when and how everything had gone so wrong. As I'd stormed away, he'd tried to call out something to me, but my brain had been too addled to hear the words.

I thought of all the books I'd read, the stories where letters went missing or were delivered too late or to the wrong person; where pride, prejudice, and accidental judgments tore lovers apart. So what had he said? It would be worth something just to know that Kieran *wanted* to make things right, if only to throw the explanations back in his face.

Midnight chimed, his sleep-time officially here. I'd set the reminder after that first night, the night of his falling asleep, of my dance in the storm.

Why hadn't he called?

I groaned with frustration, sinking lower into the water. I'd sworn an oath that I wasn't going to call him. An oath on my life, which suddenly felt as powerful as the dictates of my bioframe inside me. I'd die for sure if I broke it.

Minutes ticked away. Was he really sleeping without my voice tonight? I lay there fuming, imagining him calling Barefoot and asking her to sneeze and honk him into dreamland. Fat chance. He needed *me*. . . .

But no way was I calling him. A true heroine never breaks an oath.


His father looked surprised to see me.

"Mr. Black? I'm Maria, a friend of Kieran's."

"Oh?" He looked down at my long black dress clinging to wet skin, the water dripping from my hair.

"I'm in his Scarcity class. I need to talk to him. In *person*."

"Scarcity class . . . ?" A light went on behind the old

man's eyes, and he smiled. "Oh, yes. I believe he's mentioned you."

"Really?"

"Well, not by name." He chuckled. "But a father notices these things."

"*Things?*" I asked. His eyes widened a little, and I resolved to rein in my intensity. "Um, I know he might be asleep, but if I could just see him for a minute . . ."

"Asleep?" The man said the word like it came from another language. "Actually, he's not here at the moment."

I frowned. But it was midnight . . . and then a beautiful realization took flight in me.

He was too upset! *Unable to sleep!*

"Tossing and turning," I murmured.

"Pardon me?" his father asked.

"Where is he?" I demanded, my resolve against intensity failing.

"Perhaps you and I should have a little chat about Kieran. You're both very young, and—"

"Where . . . is . . . he?"

He paused, fear starting to show on his face. "Um, I think maybe you should go home and check your bioframe, young lady."

I growled and clenched my fists, and the old man took a step backward, setting the coats hanging along the hallway swaying.

Thick, white, puffy parkas, with fur-lined collars . . .

I smiled. "He's at the South Pole, isn't he?"

"Now, young lady . . ."

I grabbed one of the parkas and pulled it on. Then I stuffed my slippered feet into a pair of tall boots waiting by the teleporter.

"You can't go down there!" he cried. "It isn't *safe*!"

"Safe!" I laughed. "You're talking to a girl who walks in hurricanes, Mr. Black." Wobbly in my oversized boots, I stepped into the teleporter. "South Pole, please!"

"Amundsen-Scott Station?" the machine asked.

"Yes, that's the place!"

"Wait!" Kieran's father said, a trembling hand raised as if to stop me. But he came from the soft, hormone-balanced world I'd left behind, and could hardly be expected to believe that some crazy, half-drowned girl had pushed her way into his house and now was headed straight to the South Pole.

I hummed him a mad tune as I disappeared.


The feeble sun was low on the horizon. It was dark, and cold, and *white*.

I pulled the parka tighter, flipping the furry hood up over my face. On this end, the inside of the teleporter had been plastered with all kinds of warnings: climate extremes, exposure, frostbite, death. But the stickers were worn and peeling, and no calm, automated voice had asked what I was doing here. Nobody came to the end of the world unprepared, it seemed.

I climbed down the short flight of stairs; the buildings were on stilts, as if afraid to touch the snow. The wind rushed in under my dress, hit my bare knees like something *burning*.

A woman trudged by in a tempsuit and parka, pausing for a moment to stare at me with goggled eyes.

"Where's Kieran Black?" I demanded, my tongue freeze-drying in my mouth as I spoke.

"The school kid?" She paused a moment, then pointed one giant-gloved hand at an igloo a hundred meters away. "But I don't think you should be—"

I growled and turned away from her, starting a grim march past a row of flags stuck into the ice, tattered leftovers from countries that no longer existed. My dress solidified as I walked, shedding hailstones of frozen bathwater.

As the cold gripped my body, I finally believed those books where heroines died from wandering around outside. Maybe it had only taken a cold rain to kill them back then, but the Antarctic wind made the whole thing much more plausible. Every breath shredded my lungs, my wet hair making cracking noises inside the parka hood.

My bioframe was threatening to call for medical attention, but I ignored it—Kieran always bragged that emergency response took long minutes here. I kept trudging, slitted eyes focused on the distant igloo.

The hard-packed snow gave way to knee-high drifts, and snow rolled in over the tops of my boots, numbing my feet. I stumbled and was forced to pull my hands out of their warm pockets for balance. If I fell down, I'd shatter like a dropped icicle.

My brain was growing fuzzy, my heart pounding sluggishly, the world shrinking to the little tunnel of the parka hood.

Then a brilliant star flared before me . . .

A human shape was making its way around the igloo, waving a gout of flame across the curved surface of the ice. My freeze-dried brain remembered Kieran saying something about a blowtorch.

I tried to call to him, but my lungs could only suck the tiniest gulps of air, like breathing ice cubes. My body kept moving, driven forward by the promise of the glowing ember in Kieran's hands.

Fire was hot—I recalled this fact from some pre-Antarctic existence.

I staggered on until I was close enough to feel the warmth. My bare hands reached out for the flame, my fingertips slightly blue.

Kieran finally heard my snow-crunching footsteps and turned to face me, letting out a yelp of surprise.

"Maria! What are you . . . ?" The torch fell from his

hands into the snow, where it sputtered and died.

I fell to my knees beside it, groaning with disappointment. I reached for the still-glowing metal . . . and then Kieran's hands were around my shoulders, and I wanted to kill him for dragging me away from that sliver of leftover heat.

Through the tunnel of my parka hood, I watched my boots skidding across the snow until the pale sunlight darkened. Suddenly it was warm, gloriously hot, maybe even above freezing! My hood was pushed back, Kieran's concerned and goggled face in front of me, the inside walls of the igloo shimmering with artificial light.

"What are you doing here?" He pulled off his goggles and parka, stripping off his tempsuit right in front of me. "Are you crazy?"

Half naked, he wrapped the silver tempsuit around me, its elements burning my skin like hot coals. I could only nod and stare. It felt like my eyes would shatter if I blinked.

"Came see you," I managed.

"I'm so sorry," he said. "I never dreamed about Barefoot, never once! It was you from that very first night!" He swallowed. "But it was so weird and incredible, and everyone always said that dreams weren't real. But they *are* sometimes. . . . Do you know what I mean?"

"Yesh," I assured him through cracked lips. There was

more in heaven and earth and all that . . . so much more to say.

But just then, my frantic bioframe realized that I'd reached somewhere warm and safe, and so dutifully knocked me out, not wanting to risk me freezing myself again.

Stupid perfect world.

# Nine

"SO HERE WE ARE at the end of our little adventure," Mr. Solomon began.

Barefoot Tillman sneezed in her quarantine corner. She'd been much better the last couple of days; the goo had stopped running from her nose. But everyone still kept their distance.

"*Gesundheit,*" Maria said, having looked up a few old traditions on Barefoot's behalf. We smirked at each other.

"But before we all return to the modern world, perhaps we should share about our experiences." He spread his hands. "Anyone?"

Lao Wrigley raised her hand. "Well, I feel like I got much closer to my father."

"Hmm," Mr. Solomon said. "Because you made him

fly you to and from the Bahamas every day?"

"Necessity is the mother of invention." Lao flicked her hair.

"Check out these abs!" Sho cried, standing up in the front row, spinning around and lifting his shirt. "I may never eat again."

"I doubt that," Mr. Solomon said. "And I believe those are *ribs*, Mr. Walters, not muscles. Anyone else with profundities to share? Yes, Mr. Stratovaria?"

"Well," Dan said, "I've discovered that there's nothing funny about parasites."

"Ah, insight from the sightless. Someone, at least, appreciates the seriousness of scarcity. Perhaps this semester hasn't been entirely wasted."

"No kidding," Dan said, waving his cane in one white-veined hand. "My mom's so freaked out, she's shelling out big-time for the replacements. My new eyes are going to *kick ass*!"

Mr. Solomon sighed. "Indeed. And is there any great wisdom from you two lovebirds holding hands in the back?"

We pulled apart as everyone spun around, still quizzical at the two of us together. My friends blamed William Shakespeare for turning me into a meeker. They rolled their eyes at the old-speak that sometimes burbled out of my mouth.

But the changes had come from a place more primeval

than they thought. The Bard had nothing on my sub-conscious.

"Well, Mr. Solomon," Maria said, "I learned that those olden-day heroines weren't nearly as wimpy as I thought. Turns out you really can die from running around outside in the cold. Especially if you're wet." With her free hand, she pointed to the dark patch of frostbite on her left cheek, which shone like a misplaced black eye. Her mother had made Maria promise to get a skin graft soon, but in the meantime she was seriously milking it.

"Fascinating," Solomon said. "Though perhaps not as relevant to your original project as one might hope."

"Oh, I assure you, Mr. Solomon," Maria said. "Unbalanced hormones and Antarctic exposure go hand in hand."

"An interesting observation. And you, Mr. Black? What have you to tell us about the rigors of sleep?"

What indeed? I took a deep breath, wondering what I was going to do after class ended today. Now that the final projects were over, I could reset my bioframe, switch on all those little nanos that would make my anabolic and catabolic processes simultaneous once more—no need to sleep ever again.

Did I still want my dreams? They weren't so different from real life, now that Maria and I had connected out here in the waking world. But I kept wondering what else they might show me, what magic would be lost if I never twitched and blinked my way through Stage 5 again.

"I'm glad I tried it, Mr. Solomon."

"Did you make it all the way down to REM sleep?"

"You bet," I said. "Dreams, rapid-eye movement, drool, the whole deal."

Maria shot me a sly look. We'd decided not to mention that she'd dreamed once, too, courtesy of acute hypothermia, combined with a little knock-out juice from her bioframe. Or to tell Solomon that my hormones had followed hers out of balance, since modern-day widgets weren't calibrated for someone sleeping six hours a night. I'd gone mad enough to have teleported to a deluge in Denmark the night before, just to hold Maria's hand in the freezing rain.

Our projects had overlapped in all kinds of interesting ways.

"And what exactly did you dream of, Mr. Black?" Solomon asked.

Maria reached over to squeeze my hand again, fingernails biting flesh.

"Scarcity, Mr. Solomon," I said. "War, pestilence, famine. All the slings and arrows of outrageous fortune that this world does not allow."

"Really?" He raised an eyebrow. "*Nightmares* is the old term, I believe. So you must be relieved to be here at the end."

"Most definitely," I said, hearing the sound of Maria

scribbling in her notebook, tangling more words and images inspired by my lies. And I decided: no adjustments to my bioframe this afternoon, not yet.

At least one more night of dreams.

# Thinner Than Water

JUSTINE
LARBALESTIER

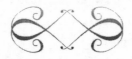

*I* WAS GOING TO RUN away, but then I saw Robbie bathing in the river.

It was a few hours shy of midnight. The village was asleep. I'd snuck out and gone walking, trying to plot how to run away. Where to go.

I took the path down to the river, ducking cobwebs glowing in the full moon, wondering how long it would take me to walk to the city. How much food I'd need. How many pairs of shoes. An owl hooted and took off just over my head. I was startled, I stumbled, and, when I righted myself, I was gazing at Robbie splashing water over his head and shoulders.

His skin shone. It was only the drops of water reflected in the moonlight and the contrast with his dark skin, but I think I forgot to breathe.

For the first time I looked at someone and wanted to touch them. My hand half lifted toward him.

"Jean!" he called, turning to me and smiling. "Jeannie."

My hand dropped to my side and the skin across my face tightened and grew hot. I wasn't dizzy, but I still wondered if I might faint. I don't think I'd ever heard him say my name before.

"Robbie," I said, stepping closer to the riverbank.

"Will you be on the hill tomorrow?"

I nodded, though I couldn't believe he was asking me. He was so . . . not beautiful or handsome, but there was something, something that made me want to touch him. I'd heard other girls talking about him.

Robbie was asking me to handfast with him. Me, who he'd never spoken to before. I shivered. I know it sounds like fancy, but I could feel my left and right ventricles squeezing blood out from my heart and into my tissues, my lungs. Robbie's words made them pump faster. Handfast? Me with him?

Tomorrow was Lammas Day. First day for bread from the new harvest. You take two fresh loaves to church as an offering—one for inside, for Jesus; and one to place outside for the fairy folk—and if you're young and not married, you can handfast. A trial wedding. If it sticks, come next Lammas Day, you make it proper. If it doesn't, you don't.

The girls sit on the hill and wait for the boys to

come ask them. I'd just agreed to sit there and wait for Robbie.

They don't handfast anywhere but the villages around here. The tourists come to watch and take photos of the couples with handkerchiefs tying them hand to hand. They think it's quaint and adorable. They think *we* are quaint and adorable.

I didn't think Robbie was quaint or adorable. I thought he was dangerous and wild, and not just because my parents didn't like him, but because there was something in the air around him, something that made me shiver. A shiver that was both warm and cold.

Lammas was the day I'd chosen to run. Because my parents had decided it was well past time for me to be 'fasted. They'd given me the whole day off. Plenty of time to get away.

"I'll see you there?" Robbie asked.

I watched the way his mouth moved, his lips, his tongue.

"Yes," I said. "On the hill."

I'd decided to stay.

On Lammas Day, the cattle tails are bound in red and blue ribbons to keep the fairy folk from stealing them. To keep them out of our houses, there are crosses above all the doors and windows. Lammas Day is when the green folk like to come calling.

Our bakery was no different, crosses nailed to all the lintels. I lived there with my ma and pa, my two brothers, Angus and Fergus, and their wives, Sheila and Maggie. All of us lived redfaced, sweaty and floured, making and baking from midnight till dawn, then over again. Before Lammas Day, the work is longer and harder as we baked enough loaves to fill every corner of hell.

It was a horrible life.

The tourists loved it. They loved us, leaving coins and notes in a tin on the front counter, large chunks of it foreign. It was my job to gather it up, sort it, and take it to the bank to turn into real money. Not to put it *in* the bank. Oh no.

My parents didn't believe in banks. Or in foreign countries. Or in anything but our little tourist-trap village, though they called it "traditional" and our ways "fitting." Our money was kept under my parents' mattress. That mattress was filled with straw. Like mine. The straw scratched.

The bakery was at the front of our house, and the living quarters in back, and up the rickety stairs, the bedrooms. There was no television, no radio, no electricity. The ovens ran on coal and wood. In the dark, we used candles and the fire of the ovens to see. In summer, we went to bed long before the sun set and in winter not long after. Summer or winter, we were always up before it rose.

My parents were obsessed with maintaining the old ways, but I read in a book that in the old days everyone made their own food. They didn't have bakeries. There weren't any tourists to feed. You only provided food for your neighbours when they came visiting.

My parents' version of the past rarely matched what my teachers told me or what I read in books. They believed in the fairy folk, the green men, and that the old ballads were history, not story. They believed in a world that stayed the same from day to day, year to year, century to century.

That tourists came to watch them be the same—day after day, week after week—didn't strike them as odd.

"Were there tourists a century ago? Two centuries?" I asked.

My ma told me I was insolent; my pa ignored me. Angus said he'd hit me if I ever said such a thing again, and Maggie giggled. We do not get on, my brothers and their wives and me.

For as long as I could remember, I've wanted to run away. I did not love my family. I didn't even like them. I wanted to live with a real family. One that would have let me stay at school past the age of fifteen. A family that would let me go to university, study to become a doctor. A family that would allow me a real life in the real world. A family that would let me leave.

My brothers didn't mind the life. Especially Angus. He liked it, couldn't wait to take over the bakery for Pa. He and Fergus saw nothing wrong with being barely educated, marrying at sixteen, having children at eighteen, staying at home where there's nothing but family and baking and church on Sunday, and, very rarely, a visit to the Green Man Tavern to yell and sing with their mates. They liked making the deliveries in a cart drawn by two old farting drays.

I don't suppose it will shock you to hear that my parents didn't hold with combustion engines.

They didn't hold with strangers, either.

Especially not Robbie.

Robbie's family hadn't lived in our village for countless generations. Because Robbie had no family.

He was found when he was wee in a cradle boat down by the shore. A fairy cradle boat, sent by the green men, everyone said, but the miller took him in anyway. He had no son of his own. But within five years, he had three and Robbie was demoted. Not a son anymore, more like a distant cousin.

He lived with the miller, his wife, his sons, and his daughters. And at harvest time, he'd bend his back in the fields along with everyone else. But he didn't work in the mill. Robbie turned to fiddling and odd jobs around the village.

Not what my parents considered marriage material.

My parents wouldn't let me leave. They wouldn't let me study. They hardly let me read. My Goldstein's *Anatomy & Physiology* had gone missing, and when I'd complained, my mother had wanted to know what I needed with it now that I was almost sixteen and out of school (they made me) and getting too old not to be married.

I had the book almost memorised, but that wasn't the point. Just having it, being able to pore over the charts and diagrams of all the systems: cardiovascular, digestive, endochrine, excretory, immune, integumentary, muscular, nervous, reproductive, respiratory, skeletal; to murmur their names ... That book was the future I wanted so desperately. The future my parents had taken away.

So why not handfast with Robbie? They wanted me tied down to someone from the village, didn't they? What did it matter if he wasn't a McPherson or a Cavendish or a Macilduy?

I hoped they wouldn't be *too* angry. And if they were, well, a handfast is not a proper marriage. It's just practice. Either one of us could walk away if we chose.

And maybe, just maybe, I could convince Robbie to run away to the city with me. He'd study music and play in the taverns. And I'd work in a shop or a pub or even a bakery, and study whenever I could. Work hard and long until they let me into a university to learn everything I could about medicine, about the ins and outs of the human body. All the secrets that weren't in Goldstein's *Anatomy & Physiology*.

I made it home before midnight and crept into bed. I thought I wouldn't sleep, thinking about Robbie and me handfasting, but I was out as soon as I closed my eyes, not even stirring when the others were up and baking.

The sun woke me. I lay there on the scratchy straw a moment, savouring the warmth being absorbed by my epidermis.

Lammas Day.

I pulled on my best dress: homespun and homemade with crooked stitching, and cloth not as scratchy as straw, but not anywhere near as soft as shop-bought cotton. One day, I told myself, I would wear a dress someone else had made.

"Are you awake, Jeannie?" my ma called.

I ran downstairs to her.

"You look nice," she said, handing me a sack and straightening my apron. "That's bread and cheese and a garland for you."

"Thank you, Ma," I said.

"Do us proud."

"I will."

I took the sack and set out for the hill to meet Fiona and wait for Robbie. The day was bright, without a hint of rain.

Fiona laughed when she saw me and waved. She was at the top of the hill. I made my way up, weaving past the other girls, nodding and smiling and exchanging hellos, avoiding eye contact with the few tourists pushy enough to take photos. I sat down next to Fi at the the crest, under the biggest ash tree, hot and a little out of breath.

"Trust you to pick the very top!" I complained.

"But look," Fi said, "you can see clear out to the ocean. And those hazy bits—I think those are the islands."

I squinted where she pointed. Everything dazzled, especially the endless blue sea blurring into endless blue sky. I grunted. "It could be." I'd prefer a view of the highway that led to the city. Or of Robbie.

"We can also see who asks who. Gossip's-eye view."

"True enough." That was why we'd come every other year. I broke the bread in half. "Did you bring a knife?"

She nodded and handed it to me. "Also pickles. Store-bought."

"Yum!" I sliced the cheese and laid it evenly on the two halves, then Fi added the pickles.

As we ate, a few boys stopped by and swapped garlands with their sweethearts. I wondered how long it would be before Robbie came to ask me, and what Fiona would say.

"Looks like Dougie and Susan are back together again."

"Who can tell with those two?" I said wisely, though

I hadn't hardly seen either since my parents pulled me out of school. I hadn't known they'd been together in the first place. Fi always promised to keep me up to date, but we barely saw each other outside of church.

"Dougie just bought a car. It's only four or five years old. I bet that's why Susan's decided she likes him again."

I felt a hot pulse of jealousy. If I had a car, I could be out of here faster than a loaf proves in summer, hopefuly with Robbie by my side. Or at least I could if someone would teach me how to drive. "Where does he keep it?" I asked. Cars and trucks and the like aren't allowed in the village. The tourists' buses park on the edge of town and they walk in, grumbling every step of the way.

"Out in the paddock with all the other cars and buses. Where else?"

I nodded, feeling foolish. He wouldn't have to hide it, would he? Dougie didn't have to hide. His parents didn't want him to be trapped in the village forever.

"How about you?" I asked, wiping my hands on my skirt. "Do you—"

Someone coughed. I looked up and had to hide my groan. Instead of Robbie it was Sholto McPherson: the boy most likely to annoy. He thinks because he's tall with blond hair, blue eyes, and clear skin every girl in the world is in love with him. Maybe some are, but not for long—half a conversation is enough to fall out of love.

"Where's your garland?" he asked.

"My what?" I asked, pulling my skirt down to hide it and hoping he would take the hint and go away. Fi giggled.

"If we're gunna handfast, we have to swap garlands first."

"We're not going to handfast."

"You what?"

"I don't want to handfast with you, Sholto. Not interested."

Sholto stared as if I was suddenly speaking the language of the cows. We'd gone through school together (until I had to leave), and in all that time I'd never said a kind word to him. He was a bully—conceited, mean, and without any sense of humour.

"Why not?"

"I don't like you, Sholto. Never have." You are no Robbie, I thought.

"Well," he said, clearly wondering if the fairy folk had possessed me. Sholto doesn't believe there's any girl who doesn't want him.

"Not even if you were a tourist. And richer than the queen."

"But—"

"Not if it was handfast with you or die." I grinned at Fiona. I was almost disappointed when he shook his head and told me I was possessed.

"You're not right," he said, walking away. Halfway

down the hill, he stopped and asked a girl I didn't recognise. She must have been from one of the other villages, but she seemed to know enough not to say yes.

Fi laughed and pinched my arm. "Well done."

"He's an idiot."

"He is. Oh, look. There's Sholto's brother, Charlie."

"What's *he* doing here?" I asked.

"His dad says he'll kill him if he doesn't find a girl soon," Fiona said.

"But he doesn't *like* girls."

"Do you think his father will take that for an answer?"

I didn't. No more than my parents would let me go back to school. "Poor Charlie."

Fiona nodded. "Poor Charlie."

"So are you planning on 'fasting with someone?" I asked to tease her.

Fi smiled. "I'm just here to watch. Like always. Can you imagine what my parents would do?"

Fiona's parents weren't like mine. They had a car and a radio—and a television. When I was little, I used to sneak over to watch it sometimes. Stories of girls living lives nothing like mine. It was the first time I saw what a doctor was and that I could grow up to be one. Or I could if I'd been born somewhere else to different parents.

Fiona's parents wanted her to go to university in the city where her mum's parents lived. They thought fifteen was too young for handfasting or marriage. And sixteen and seventeen and eighteen, too. Her dad had grown up in the village, but he'd gone away and come back with a wife and plans to bring more tourists and all sorts of beliefs that did not match my parents'.

There were others like them who just pretended to be quaint for the tourist money. They liked the surface of the old ways, not their guts. Unlike my parents, folks like Fiona's family didn't believe in fairies or in girls being married before they were old enough to know what they wanted out of life.

But there weren't enough of them; my parents' way was still the majority way. It was changing, but not quick enough for me.

"You're lucky," I told her.

Fiona didn't say anything. What could she say? She knew it.

"My garland's drooping." I pulled it out from under my skirt and dropped it in her lap.

"It is. Does this mean *you're* here to handfast?" Her voice wobbled, as if she was trying to sound happy for me when really she was sad. I wished Robbie would hurry up.

Fiona was afraid of me becoming a child bride. Lots of the tourists look at us like that. Once one of them asked me how I could stand it. I told her lies about how happy I was and how wonderful and fitting and pure and traditional our ways were and how I didn't want any other life.

That tourist girl had short hair. No heavy cord of plait down past her arse. She wasn't wrapped in too long skirts and scratchy shirts. I'd wanted to hit her. Or find a way to steal her life.

And now Fiona was looking at me the same way that tourist had. She felt sorry for me. Where was Robbie? *He* didn't feel sorry for me.

"I might handfast," I said and then when Fi's face twisted, "I might not."

"Shall we make another garland then?" she asked. "There are enough daisies about."

"How long have you got?"

"Till dinner," Fiona said, meaning noon. "And after that, I said I'd help with the shop. You can come if you like. I've got a whole stack of new magazines."

"Sounds nice," I said.

We plucked all the daisies around us and then dug our nails through the stems, making a chain. The juice from the stems stained our fingers and gave them that slightly sticky, sweet smell of summer.

"It's not as bad as you think it is," I told her, thinking of Robbie with his dark skin and green eyes, wishing he would come.

"No," Fiona murmured, plucking and threading daisies.

But it was too late. The gulf that had opened up between us when I'd left school and she hadn't, well, I could feel it grow bigger with every flower added to our chains. Fiona packed away her pickles and knife and said goodbye long before noon.

I watched her go, and then the bustling and toing and froing of the villagers, the handfasters, the tourists. But where was Robbie? I turned back to the daisies, plucking and threading them together. The chains piled up beside me.

Had he been teasing me last night? But it hadn't seemed that way. Had I wasted this chance to escape? I was just the smallest fraction away from despair when a voice startled me.

"That's a lot of daisy chains."

"It is," I said, looking up. His eyes were so green. "I'm going for the world record. How many do you reckon I've got?"

"I couldn't guess—a girl as nimble as you could make a dozen while I stand blinking the sun from my eyes."

"Is that so? A dozen a second? Then I don't have nearly enough. I've been here all morning."

Robbie sat down beside me. I looked at him sideways, not meeting his eyes. His fiddle was slung across his back and his curly black hair was tied back with a piece of leather. I could feel how close he was to me, almost smell his sweat.

"Sitting idle playing with flowers. How many days are there like these?" he asked. I couldn't tell if he was looking at me. I was bent over daisy-chaining, piercing and threading.

"Oh, not nearly enough. And this one's more than half gone. Tomorrow it's back to the bakery." Air exploded out of me in a sigh. Was he going to ask me or not?

"It's not so bad, is it?" He picked up a handful of daisy chains and told off the flowers one by one as if they were rosary beads.

I didn't know how to answer. "I don't like it," I said, because it was as mild as I could be. Not the bakery, not this village, not this life. I wanted to be elsewhere. Learning, living, growing. Not covered in flour and making quaint to tourists.

"I love it here." He said it softly and—I glanced to check—he was still smiling, but the words made my heart slip a little. I'd hoped he was as desperate to get away as me.

"Really? But they're all so . . ." Most of the village shunned him, said his green eyes were too like the fairy folk. Never mind that half the village has green eyes. In some lights, mine are green, too.

He shrugged, then turned to me just as I looked up. There. Him looking at me; me looking at him.

I held my breath. He *was* going to ask me.

He didn't look away. I noticed the bumps on his nose.

It must have been broken once. More than once. There was a scar, too, below his left eye. I'd never looked at him so close before. I let my breath out. "And where were you, Master Robbie? I've waited an age!"

He laughed. "Building a house."

Now I laughed. "You never!"

"We have to live somewhere. The mill is crowded." He leaned a little closer. There was a light film of sweat above his upper lip. "I'm glad last night was real. I was afraid I'd dreamed it. Even though I never slept."

"Not a dream." I was the first to look away, down at my hands stained green from the daisies.

"I like how pale your skin is. Even your freckles are light." Robbie put the mess of flowers down and reached for my hand. "Will you 'fast with me?"

The words that had circled my ears and my heart all that day were said.

I looked up at his eyes, green and sharp as jealousy, and I couldn't think of anything but him. He leaned toward me and our mouths touched and our arms twined. The feeling of him, the smell, the taste; I thought I would explode.

I never said *yes* out loud, but we went hand in fist, and that evening found him with me at my family's hearth, and cloth binding our hands, and our year together had begun.

Neither my mother nor my father nor Angus nor

Fergus nor their brides smiled. Their faces were like stone. But they didn't stop us.

Here's what was said about Robbie in the village: They said he was a fine, fine musician.

And that was true.

When he played, the whole set of his face altered and the look of his eyes was from another country. Somewhere far from here. We have some of the best fiddlers in the land, but not like Robbie, not like him at all. It was almost as if his soul were in his fingers when he played. Impossible not to cry when he played the ballads; impossible not to dance for his jigs. He was the finest I ever heard.

Too fine, they said.

They muttered that he only cut his nails on Sundays. Old Nick that made him and surely, they said, that's where the skill in his fingers comes from. And who ever saw eyes that green in someone with skin that dark?

They said that we would never last. Not even a year.

Our first night together was difficult. It wasn't that the house he built was unfinished. In twelve hours he'd built a hut with a roof, four walls, a floor, and gaps for windows and a door. Even a rough fireplace. I wondered if the fairy folk had helped. Even the mattress wasn't any worse than what I was used to.

It wasn't the house; it was babies.

I didn't want any.

We'd come through the doorway kissing. My mouth on his; tongue and lips and teeth. I could feel the hotness of it—of him, of us—in waves through my sympathetic nervous system. My hands were on his shirt, feeling the outline of his back, and then his shirt was gone and I was feeling his skin. He was tugging at my dress, pulling it up, and his hands were on my thighs and the feeling was so intense I let out a noise, and then caught myself, grabbed his wrists.

"No, Robbie," I said, forcing the words out.

He stared at me. "No? But we're 'fasted."

"I know. We are." I let go of him, sat down on the mattress. There wasn't anywhere else. No chairs. Just a wooden box with his things in it and a sack with mine. He sat down beside me. Too close.

Both ventricles were pumping faster than they ever had. I was panting. I wondered if it was always like this. Did desire always make your heart burst?

"I can't have babies."

"You can't? Really?" He looked at me sadly. "I've always wanted children."

I took a deep breath. His thigh was against mine. I could feel it through the layers of rough homespun dress and trousers. His shirt was on the floor. "I mean I don't want to have babies."

"Not ever?" He was shocked.

"Not now. I'm too young. And I don't want to stay here—"

"But we've just 'fasted! Why did you say yes if you don't want—"

"I do want! I do. I want to be with you. We can leave together. I want to go back to school. I want to study hard and do well. I want to go to university in the city. I want to be a doctor."

"A doctor?" Robbie said as if I'd just said I wanted to be a mountain.

"Yes, but if we, you know. And if I . . ." Why was I too embarrassed to say the words "pregnant" or "sex"? If I became a doctor, I'd have to say them all the time. I blushed. I could explain physiologically what caused the blush: dilation of the small blood vessels in the face, leading to increased blood flow—but I couldn't make it stop.

"You don't want to go at it because you don't want to be expecting 'cause that'll keep you from being a doctor? Is that what you're saying?" He smiled, but it was lopsided.

I nodded.

"You know there are ways—"

"Yes," I said, my cheeks still hot. "But they're not reliable. Or if they are, we can't get them." As far as I knew, no one in the village was on the pill. Most of them probably didn't know such a thing existed. The chemist was three villages over and he would not prescribe something he did not believe in.

"So what are you saying, Jeannie? Are you saying you won't kiss me?" He leaned forward and put his lips against mine and my heart started pumping hard, left and right ventricles both.

"Yes," I breathed, pressing my lips against his. There are more nerve endings in the lips than almost any other part of the human body.

"Yes, you won't, or yes you will?"

"Yes, I'll kiss you," I said, kissing his upper lip and then his lower. His mouth opened just a little. I felt his tongue against mine.

We kissed deeper. His hands were on my face, then in my hair, down my back. I could feel both where they were now and where they'd been.

"Oh," I said.

I'd never felt like this. So heated. So overcome. So wanting. He was pushing the skirt of my dress up.

"Robbie," I whispered.

"Just to touch," he said. He leaned over and kissed my bare thigh, then looked up at me, grinning. "Can't plant any seeds with just touching."

But it can make you want to.

All night, we touched, getting close, pushing away, exhausting ourselves. It was past dawn when we finally slept.

The next morning Robbie told me that he would wait. "I'll never make you do anything you don't want."

"You promise?"

"I promise," he said, running his fingers down my cheek. I shivered. "But I can't promise that I won't complain about it." He smiled. "You're serious? It's what you want?"

"To be a doctor. Yes." I'd never wanted anything else. Except for him, and he was a very new want.

"To leave?"

"Yes!" I could imagine the freedom of the city. A place where not everyone you met knew where you lived, where you worked, who your parents were, and all your other kin.

"Well, then I'll have to come with you," he said slowly. "All I've ever wanted is to play my fiddle and find a likely lass. Now I've found her. I suppose I can play there as well as I can here."

"There's music in the city, Robbie. Lots of it. But I bet none is as good as yours."

He laughed. "How could it be? None of those fiddlers have Old Nick in their back pocket!"

So at night, we'd hold each other. We'd kiss, we'd touch, we'd twine, but nothing more, no matter how much we wanted to. During the day, Robbie took on more work:

sold tickets to the tourists, played for them, mended the McKenzies' fences, the doors of the church, anything he was offered.

They didn't let me back in my old class, so no sitting next to Fiona. They stuck me in with kids a year younger than me.

I didn't care. I worked harder than they did. My old teacher started loaning me books again, and this time I didn't have to hide them. She gave me another copy of Goldstein's *Anatomy & Physiology*—the book my ma had taken away. I wasn't going to lose it twice.

I was going to graduate. I was going to go to university. I didn't care that in the history of our school only two students had made it to university and neither of them earned a degree. I would be different. Me and Fiona both.

Robbie said he'd never met anyone like me. When I talked about university, about the city, he'd just stare as if it was impossible to imagine. Once he said, "And when you're a doctor, you'll come back here, won't you?"

That was our first fight. I couldn't understand how he could love this place; he couldn't understand my hate.

"They loathe you," I said. On our way back from church that morning, the Macilduy boys had spat at Robbie's feet. He walked on as if nothing had happened.

"Not all of them."

"They think you're one of the fairy folk."

"They're just jealous."

"Look what they did to your face," I said, touching his nose, the scar under his eye. It was a guess, but he flinched. "No one would treat you like that in the city."

"You don't know that," Robbie said, picking up his fiddle and walking out the door.

We did not sit with my family in the kirk. We were not invited to sup with them. It was months before Ma came to visit. She made sure Robbie was out.

"Look how small your cottage is," she said, sitting down on the chair Robbie had made. I sat on the mattress. "You could have better."

"I like it." Robbie was at work on another chair and a cabinet, too, so we'd have somewhere to put the proper shop-bought plates and cutlery Fiona's family had given us. They had little "Made in China" stickers on them. I'd never owned anything that came from so far.

"He's not good enough for you."

"I like him." Every day I liked Robbie a little bit more. He didn't just make me tingle, he also made me laugh.

"He'll beat you."

I snorted, then flinched, waiting for her to belt me. Then I realised it was my own home; she couldn't touch me. "It's not Robbie that's violent." I thought of his nose, his cheek.

"Just wait and see."

"Dó you want some tea?" We didn't have a stove yet, but the fireplace wasn't smoking as much as it had. "It won't take long."

Ma shook her head. "And why are you back in school?"

"I like school."

"And he lets you go?"

I realised Ma hadn't said Robbie's name. Not once.

"Did you hear that the McKenzies' cows have sickened?"

I had. "And the Cowans', too."

"Isn't he working for the McKenzies? Fixing their fences?"

"What of it?" I asked, enjoying my defiance. Facing her in my own house gave me strength. "Cows get sick sometimes."

"People are talking," Ma said, smiling for the first time. It wasn't hard to figure out who was talking. My family at the forefront.

"That's what people do." And sometimes what they say isn't vicious.

"You'd better hope they don't die."

"The people?" I asked.

"No, the cows."

"Cows die all the time."

Ma sucked her teeth. "What if you have a baby?" she asked, pulling a package of herbs from her pocket and handing it to me. "This will keep you free."

After she left, I buried them next to the wild primroses in the vegetable garden I'd started. Two days later,
the primroses were dead.

The next time, my mother came with a loaf of barley
bread. She looked tired. More tired than usual. I pushed
my books aside so she could put the loaf on the table
Robbie had just finished. She sighed as she collapsed
into the chair. "Are you going to stay with him past the
year?"

I pulled up the other chair. "Of course," I said. I was
happy. There was Robbie and my studies—the day before
I'd been moved forward a year. I was back sitting next to
Fiona.

Ma started crying.

I had never seen my mother cry before. I patted her
shoulder.

"I love you," she said. She'd never said that before,
either. I'd seen television shows at Fiona's place where
parents told their children that they loved them, but I'd
never seen it in real life. I didn't know what I was supposed to say.

"What's wrong, Ma?"

"Just promise me that at the end of the handfasting
you won't make it a proper marriage."

"I can't promise you that. I love him." It was true I
realised, though I hadn't told Robbie yet.

"You're not pregnant, are you?"

I shook my head, but I didn't tell her there was no chance of that. I didn't want her to know anything about what happened—or *didn't*—between these walls.

"Well, I tried," she said, wiping her eyes, standing up.

"What do you mean 'you tried'?"

"To tell you that you'd be better off without him."

"But I'm better off *with* him. I'm happy. I've never been happy before."

Ma stared at me, her eyes red from her tears. "He's fairy folk, you know that, don't you? He's not right."

"Oh, Ma." I sighed. How could she believe that? "Green eyes don't mean anything. You've got green eyes."

"Not like his," she said, shaking her head. "You don't believe, but you should. Look at this place. It even smells of fairy. Your father wants you home. He'll wait till your handfasting's done, but only if you promise."

"Promise what?"

"That you won't make it a proper marriage."

She still wouldn't say Robbie's name. "No, I won't promise. At the end of the year, I'll marry Robbie for real. That's what I want." And to leave this horrible village.

"That's a mistake."

I didn't say anything.

"You're sure?"

"Yes," I said.

"I'll be off then," Ma said, standing up.

"So soon? Don't you want a cup of tea? Scones? I made them myself," I said, pointing to the oven Robbie had cobbled together.

She shook her head. "No, no. I've got to get back to the bakery. It's just Pa on his own. And four busloads of the gawkers on their way."

She raised her hand and touched my cheek. Something else she'd never done before.


Later, I found out that Fiona had come to warn us, but she was too late. My family and a mob behind them got to our cottage first.

We were kissing. My hands were under his shirt and his were on my waist. I was wishing there was some way to have babies but still finish school and go to university and become a doctor.

Robbie murmured in my ear, his words blurring together so that all I could hear was want.

"I love you," I told him. Later, I was so glad of those words.

"And I love you, Jeannie," he answered, looking straight into my eyes, brushing his hand over my lips. "Always."

That's when they started hammering on the door.

We leapt up. Robbie pulled me close.

My father, Angus, and Fergus came through the door.

Behind them, I could see my mother, Sheila and Maggie, more than half the village. A few carried torches. My father carried an axe.

"What?" Robbie and I said together. I squeezed closer against him, held on to his arms across my chest.

"There's a meeting," my pa said. "We'd like you to come." He was looking at Robbie, not me.

"Thank you kindly for the invitation," Robbie said, holding me tighter. "But tonight I have other plans."

I nodded, knowing that if I spoke, my voice would shake too much to get the words out.

"You'll come with us," Pa said.

"Pa-a-a?" I stammered. "I want him to stay." My voice squeaked.

"Come on, Jeannie," Angus said, all holier than thou. "Let him go. We're doing this for you."

"Doing what exactly?" Robbie asked, his voice steady. "I see no need to leave my home."

"Just take him," Fergus said.

The three of them stepped forward. We stepped back. Held on to each other tighter.

"No," I said. I'd meant to yell, but my throat was too tight.

Angus grabbed at me. I let go of Robbie and started flailing my arms. I tried to form fists, but my panic went against me. I think I landed a kick or two to Angus's shins. I wished I was wearing shoes.

There were more men in the room now. I saw Sholto McPherson and his father, the Macilduy boys, the McAndrewses, Cavendishes, and McKenzies, too. They were pulling Robbie away from me and me from him. He punched and kicked, but there were too many of them.

"Let him go!" I yelled, but I couldn't hear my words. There were so many people yelling, grabbing, swearing. Plates smashed. Wood broke.

They dragged him outside, spitting at him, kicking. He gave back as good as he got. I saw blood on his face. "Robbie!"

My arms were pinned behind me. Sholto McPherson and Fergus were struggling to grab my legs. I got Sholto square in the face. My toes hurt like hell, but it was worth it. I hoped I'd broken his nose.

"Robbie!" I couldn't see him now.

"Hush, girl," my ma said. Sheila and Maggie beside her. "You go now, Angus, Fergus, Sholto. We've got her."

As soon as they let go, I bolted for the door, but Ma was right, she had me. She and the in-laws knocked me flat to the floor and held me there.

"Let me go, Ma. Let me go to him."

I tried to push up, but Maggie was sitting on my legs. She was grinning. "Shouldn't have 'fasted with a demon, should you?"

"He's not a demon."

"Take the smile off your lips, Maggie," Ma said. "It's not a laughing matter."

Maggie said nothing, but her eyes were smiling. If Sheila and Ma weren't holding my shoulders down I'd have scratched those eyes out.

"What are they doing to him?" I asked, slowly. It was hard to get the words out without tears escaping, too. I would not cry in front of them.

"Judging," Ma said. "It will be done fair."

I doubted that. I closed my eyes and bit the inside of my cheeks. "What will happen to him?"

"What he deserves."

"And what will that be?" He deserves to be with me far away from this place, but that was not what they'd give him.

"Can you keep her down, girls? I think I'll make us tea."

I don't know how long it was before Fergus came and talked to Ma in whispers. Hours it felt like. Months. They'd let me up. I was curled into a ball on the mattress, staring at the cabinet full of broken plates, listening to the whispering, but failing to pick out any of the words. I was trying hard not to think, not to imagine. I couldn't bear the thought of what they'd done.

"There's something we have to show you," Ma said at last, turning to me.

I stood up, feeling every bruise they'd given me. I

pulled my shawl around my shoulders, but it did nothing to keep me warm.

They walked me down to the river: my ma, Sheila, and Maggie and Fergus, hand in hand, as if we were out on an excursion to find night-flowering catchfly. I half expected them to start skipping. If I could have killed them, I would have.

"It's just ahead," Fergus said.

"You can't make a fuss," my mother said, turning to me. "Or they'll do the same to you."

I saw a pile of rags. Half in the river, half out.

It wasn't rags. The tightness in my throat grew and spread. I knelt beside him. His head and shoulders were in the water. He didn't move.

"But Robbie didn't hurt anyone," I said softly. I untied his hands, wrenched up high behind his back. The bonds were wet and hard to shift. His fingers were swollen and broken. His arms, too. I pushed at his body, trying to turn it over. I was panting now, and wet.

He did not look like Robbie. His nose was beaten so bad it was smeared across his face. His eyes were dull. No green at all. And his skin was pale as it had never been; as if there was no blood circulating below. He didn't smell like Robbie, either. They'd driven my Robbie away.

"He was a devil," Ma said. "A witch."

"He was my husband. My love."

"Only a handfasting," she said. "Nothing real. He

bewitched you is all." She slid her arm through mine and pulled me up from the water. I was too numb to shake her off. I couldn't cry. I couldn't scream. It was all frozen inside me.

"He had green eyes," Ma continued. "And the way he played. Well, it wasn't right. No one knows who his father is. Or his mother. You know the McKenzies' cows died? Right after he built those fences."

This wasn't real. Nothing like it ever happened on any of the television I'd seen with Fiona, nor in the books and magazines we'd read together. Not now. Not in this world. This country.

They were all mad.

Why had I been born in this village? Fewer than a hundred miles from the city, but more than a hundred years away.

They took me to the church and dunked me in holy water. I think some were sad to see no hiss of steam, no water bubbling from the heat of my skin that had been so close to his.

"Poor pet to be fastened hand in hand to a demon. Lucky lass to be freed and untainted."

If I'd been strong enough, I would have spat at them, kicked and punched and screamed.

I had no strength left. All I could do was beg them to let me bury my Robbie.

My ma intervened, so they allowed it, but not in the churchyard, and no marker on top.

Fiona, her mother, and her father wielded the shovels with me.

Fiona was crying. Her mother, too. I wished they'd stop. It made my eyes sting. They kept telling me things, and I was listening, but I couldn't take any of it in. Their words floated over me.

My eyes were mostly down, watching the dirt hit Robbie's chest, his legs, his arms, his bloodless ruined face. But worst of all was when he was covered over: There was no him left, only dirt.

Afterward, Fiona and her parents dragged me farther into the woods and then out to the paddock. I didn't ask where we were going. I could barely see. My mind was stuck on Robbie facedown in the river. Robbie with the ground on top of him. I tried to remember him laughing and his smile, when his eyes were still green, but all I could see was his crushed nose, broken fingers, the rope burns around his wrists.

"Damn it!" Fiona's father was yelling.

I was in their car. Fiona beside me. Her mother in the front turning the key, but nothing was happening. Outside, the sun was rising. I could see fields on either side.

"What?" I asked.

"The car's broken," Fiona said, getting out. I followed.

Her father was crouched over the front, swearing. "Try it again!" he called.

"I'm so sorry," Fiona told me. I wasn't sure what she was sorry about. Robbie? The car? The village?

"Me, too," I said.

Her father slammed the hood shut. He nodded at me. "I'm sorry, Jeannie, we're going to have to turn it around, wheel it back to town. Dougie can take a look. He's a wizard with engines. We'll get you out of here when it's fixed," he told me. "I promise. We're not going to forget you."

"I wish you could stay with us," Fiona said. "You know, until the car is fixed."

I nodded. That was impossible. There was already too much bad blood between her people and my parents.

"I'll stay in the cottage," I said, trying not to think of what had happened there. "I think there's enough money to see me through the end of the school year." I had never lived alone, but the cottage was mine. Every plank of wood had been touched by Robbie. I *needed* to be there.

"Oh," Fiona said, looking down. We were sitting in her kitchen. Her parents had gone to open up their shop. We still had another hour before school started.

"Oh?"

"The cottage. They—"

"What did they do?"

"It's gone, Jeannie. They tore it down. Smashed it."

This time, I cried, seeing Robbie as broken as the cottage.

My ma came for me in the middle of the first class of the day. Sheila and Angus's little Tommy was down with colic and there wasn't anyone to tend to him.

I was excused.

I walked by her side and said not a word. I didn't touch her, either. I vowed I wouldn't touch or speak to any of them.

My ma didn't say anything about my moving back into the bakery, but there was a sack of my things on my old bed. No books, no money, nothing Robbie had given me in it, just clothes.

They woke me at midnight to help with the baking. And when it was time for school, I had to mind Tommy again.

I worked hard at the dough, shaping and kneading and fighting it into bread.

At the end of the week, I walked over to Fiona's. The car was still broken. Dougie didn't know what to make of it. He'd ordered some new parts, so maybe next week.

I couldn't wait till then. Fiona gave me money, her aunt's address in the city, food and water, and her bicycle.

It blew a tire not a mile out. I put it beside the road and unhooked the pack to carry over my shoulder. I took two steps and collapsed with the most awful pain in my side.

My father found me and carried me back to the bakery. The midwife came, said I was wrung dry and thirsty (exhausted and dehydrated, a real doctor would have said). I was in bed the rest of the day drinking water, peeing in a pot, and hating my family and the village.

Fiona's parents bought another car. This time, my father, Angus, and Fergus found me before we'd left the paddock. They didn't ask where we were going. They just stood in front of the car like oak trees. Their faces didn't move. They didn't respond to anything Fiona's father said to them.

I followed them home in silence.

Then it was summer again, and Lammas Day once more. There was me, almost seventeen, already a widow, no closer to leaving this place than I'd ever been. A year from now, Fiona would know if she'd gotten into university. She might be living in the city already. And I'd still be here.

I agreed to handfast with Charlie McPherson because I could not stand another night in my parents' house. Besides, he didn't want to touch me any more than I wanted to touch him. He didn't like girls; I didn't like anyone who wasn't Robbie.

Charlie was a good, kind man. Handfasting with me kept us both safe. Though we lived close to his family, we didn't live with them. His father was so thrilled to see Charlie with a girl, he helped him build a cottage. It wasn't like the old cottage. There were four rooms, not one, and there was no grace to its walls or windows. Still, it was better than the bakery and I was spared having to break bread with his vain, murderous idiot brother Sholto each morning.

Life smoothed itself down and moved on. Charlie and I saved all the money we earned tending to the tourists. Turned out he was as keen to leave as me. When we got to the city, we'd work whatever jobs we could find and go back to school. Charlie was quick with numbers and wanted to do something—anything—that would keep him surrounded by them every day. A mathematics teacher, maybe. He didn't care. He wasn't Robbie, or even Fiona, but I liked him. And I knew he'd had no part in Robbie's death. Not like his brother or father or half the men in the village.

The sadness round my heart began to ease. Just a little.

Somewhere that easing was marked, and on the next Lammas Day, when I was seventeen, two years removed from that fine summer's day when Robbie had sat beside me and asked that I go hand in hand with him, on that day, my Robbie, he walked back into the village.

I was coming back from the well, jug in one hand, Maggie and Fergus's firstborn, Bonnie, resting on my hip, when I saw him. He walked toward me, taller than I remembered, his clothes far finer. I gasped. My mouth opened. It closed. The image was there of him on my retinas, but my brain could make no sense of it.

"Robbie?"

His nose was straight. The scar on his cheek gone. Bonnie squirmed against my side, trying to pull my hair with her sticky fingers. How could it be Robbie?

He walked directly to me. Stood less than a foot away. Nobody shouted, or tried to stop him, or stone him. No one else was gasping. No one looked his way. He was a ghost.

Silence like a fog descended on the village. Everyone's movements slowed, then stilled altogether. Bonnie stopped reaching for my hair. Spittle hung from her lip, but did not fall.

"You're . . ." I began, not knowing how to frame my questions. I wanted to put the baby down, hurl myself into his arms.

Robbie stared back at me. There was a faint greenness to his skin as if he had been unwell.

I placed the jug on the ground and put my brother's

unmoving baby beside it.

"Your body is false," he said, "but your face is fair. It didn't take you long, did it, to find yourself someone else? And a baby, too."

"A baby?" I asked, confused. "She's not my baby, Robbie. She's my brother's. Why are you talking so strange?" What are you?"

"Where I have been, Jeannie, I could have taken a noble lady, a queen, for my wife. But I couldn't forget my Jeannie and the vows we made."

"Where you've been, Robbie? You are—you were—dead. I saw your body. I buried you." My eyes stung. I could still see him lying in his grave. His broken face and fingers. And here he was without even a bump on his nose. I wanted to touch him, move closer, smell him, see if this was my Robbie.

"I despised her riches, her pearls, her furs, her light. I despised her sweet self because there was nothing in my heart but getting back to you. But you're not a maid now, eh?"

"I am."

"You are?" he said, his tone hard and unbelieving. "You're married again. They told me."

"To Charlie McPherson. You remember Charlie?"

"You're saying you waited for me? Kept yourself intact?" He was angry.

"I never wronged you," I told him. "You were dead. I

buried you. Six feet under and no flowers on top."

"What's the soil but a path to the kingdom below?"

I sat down or, rather, my legs gave way beneath me. "The kingdom below?"

"Where the fair folk are. Where their king and queen rule. It was their queen that wanted me."

The fair folk. The green ones. Fairies. Faerie. All the things my parents believed and I wanted to be educated away from. "They're under the ground? The fairy folk?" I put my hand in the dirt, got it under my fingernails, waited for something to reach up for me.

Robbie crouched down, leaned closer. He smelled of it, the dirt. His eyes were bigger than they had been. And much much greener. I reached out to touch his hand. It was warm, as if the blood still circulated beneath the layers of his skin. I had been expecting cold. His skin against mine—epidermis to epidermis—it made me feel the way I had when he was alive: want.

He leaned even closer. His lips were almost touching mine. His breath smelled like the earth. I wanted to kiss him.

"I could kill you," he said. He put his hands on either side of my head. "I'm much stronger now. I could crush your skull."

"I love you," I said, glad that my voice did not shake.

"That was the last thing you said to me before they dragged me away."

It wasn't. My last word to him was his name screamed as loud as my cracking voice would allow.

"Was it any truer then than it is now?" he asked, his hands increased their pressure on the sides of my head.

"It was always true, Robbie. It will always be true. More than two years you were under there." A tear slid down my cheek.

"Four weeks to me. A month ago you were with me."

"Four weeks?" I said. He was eighteen when they killed him; he was eighteen now. While I was almost that age myself.

"You got yourself another husband."

I shook my head. "Charlie McPherson! He's not a real husband."

"You forgot all about me."

"It's not—"

"Not what, my love? Not true? The child on the grass is not yours? The ring on your finger belongs to some other girl?"

"Bonnie is not mine. Why don't you listen? And my husband . . . Charlie! Remember Charlie? He has no interest in girls. I'm as much a maid as the day . . . " I paused. "As the day they killed you."

"Our vows are tattered and all forgot?" Robbie said softly. He was reciting a speech, not listening to me. He smiled, but it was just lips and teeth. "You took another. You have a child."

"I don't! I didn't. Look at her! Look at her hair! At her squinty little eyes. She's the image of her mother, Maggie. No child of mine would look like that."

"Why couldn't you have waited?" His hands pressed firmly on the sides of my skull. I wondered which part would break first if he began to squeeze. How fast would I die?

"Waited! You were dead, Robbie. I held you broken in my arms. Your nose was smeared across your face. Your eyes went dull. My father, my brothers, Sholto McPherson, his father, even the priest—all those hideous, righteous men. They killed you."

"They did," he agreed, listening at last. "They cursed and spat on my dying body that they'd already battered with their feet and hands and stones."

"Then why are you warm now? Did you swear your soul away to get another life?"

"No," Robbie said. "After I was dead, I sank into the earth until I slid out into her kingdom; all my bones knitted, my skin unbroken."

"Your old scars are gone. The bumps on your nose." I touched my fingers to his now-straight one. I could feel the strength in his hands. It would not take much effort for him to crush me.

"Down there they all have green eyes."

"Are they your kin?"

He nodded. "It was true what they said: I am fey. I am

a witch, an elf, kin to Faerie."

"Maybe they're your kin because they're dead like you. When you kill me," I said, daring him, but terrified he'd take my dare. "I'll be kin, too."

For a moment the pressure of his hands on my skull increased. I swallowed my screams. Then he laughed and slid his left hand to my cheek. "I'm as warm as you are."

I let out a sigh. He would not kill me yet. "You don't smell the way you used to," I told him.

"It will wash off."

Robbie sank all the way to his knees.

"I served the queen for four weeks, and each day she asked me to be hers and each day I said no. Then she let me go. They told me that you would not stay faithful."

"They were wrong."

"They told me I'd return to you and you'd be with another man and there'd be a child. They told me you'd forget my name. I laughed at them but not as hard as they laughed at me." His voice dropped. "They don't lie, you see. They *can't* lie."

Like the ballads said, and yet they'd told him nothing but lies. "They were wrong. I never forgot your name, Robbie. Not a day's gone by I haven't thought of you. I have no child, and I'm handfasted to a man who will never touch me. I've never been with anyone but you."

"You did not wait."

"I will *never* be with anyone else. I ran away from this

place as often as I could. All I want is to get away from them and everything they did to you. I've tried to run. This place won't let me go."

"Yes," he said. "They put a geas on you. You can't leave, no matter how fast you run. Your path is blocked."

"What? A geas?" I knew that word. Why couldn't I remember what it meant?

"Your parents. They used my blood to keep you here. As long as I was below the ground, you couldn't leave." Robbie stood up, pulled me up beside him, and smiled his hard smile again. My hand was in his. "Walk with me."

I walked beside him. Numb. My parents had used magic—Robbie's blood—to keep me from leaving. I had thought my hatred for them could not grow. Fiona's parents' broken car, the bicycle, the pain in my side. All of it, my parents' doing.

We walked out of the village, past the paddock and the tourist buses. A gaggle of them were frozen, some with their cameras pointed back at the village, the others out to sea.

He led me to the edge of the cliff. The ocean roared below. There was no wind. The seagulls above were frozen in air.

"They killed you to keep me here," I said.

Robbie laughed. "Oh no. They wanted me dead for my own sake. The geas was them being canny. Why waste all that fey blood?"

"I will kill them."

He laughed. "I'll help you."

I put my hand on his chest and couldn't feel his heart beating. I touched his throat where there was no pulse. "You're warm," I said.

"And green. And dead to this world."

I leaned forward so my lips were close to his. The air between us went taut. I could feel the warmth of his mouth, but no movement of his breath. I smelt only the earth. Yet I wanted him.

"Do you believe me now about Bonnie? Charlie?" I asked, staring into his too-green eyes.

He smiled. The first smile that was like my Robbie of old. "She did not have much of the look of you. And I do remember Charlie. I liked him for being almost as outcast as me."

"Good," I said. "The fairy folk are liars."

"They can't lie."

"But they can misdirect, can't they? They can confuse. Isn't that how they trick the heroes in the ballads? They told you something that isn't a lie, but isn't true, either, not all-the-way true. They didn't say I had a child, now did they? Only that you'd find me with one."

Robbie nodded.

"I've never lied to you, never told you anything that wasn't true down to its core."

"No," he said, touching my cheek. "I had forgotten

that. They can make you forget."

"We never did much together," I said at last, stepping closer to him.

"We kissed. We held each other," Robbie said, his lips moving close to mine. "Touched each other all over."

I nodded. "I thought that I would explode."

He laughed. "I did. You did. Over and over again. You drove me mad."

"I had to. I couldn't be a wife and mother, not without giving up my dreams. I never wanted any of it. Except with you."

"But later, you said. After you were a doctor."

"Yes, but they took our later away, didn't they?"

"Not entirely, Jeannie, my love. Where I've been, there's pearls, there's silk, velvet, and gold. More books than I've ever seen before. All yours, if you walk with me. If you remember our vows. All you have to do is follow me." He looked out to sea, took a step closer to the edge, pulled me with him.

"You want me as dead and gone from this world as you?"

"Yes." He smiled broader, wilder. "We'd be together. It's so much lovelier than this world."

His lips touched mine. It felt electric. Bigger than our kisses of old. He was without a heart, without a pulse, but I wanted him as much as I had when I first saw him bathing in the river.

"Why would you stay here, Jeannie? Leave your family. You never loved them, they never loved you. Come with me. Learn from the green folk. They have more learning than anyone in this world. They'll teach you whatever you want to know. You can be a doctor down there more easily than you could up here.

"Their world is as vast as this one. We'll explore it together."

"But, I'm not fey, Robbie. How do you know they'll take me the way they took you?"

"You're all fey," he said. "Some more than others, and some much less, but there isn't a person in this village— in any of these villages—without at least a drop of their blood."

I wanted to dispute him, but my parents had cast a geas. And I could feel the rightness of what he said. Fiona and her family had never gone directly against my parents. Never breathed a word about going to authorities outside the village. They knew. I knew. The rules in the village aren't the same as the world outside. Because they're fey. We're fey. I am fey.

"In some lights," Robbie said, "your eyes are green. They're already a little way toward where they'll be.

"Come with me, Jeannie." He pulled me closer to him. I felt his love, I felt his need. I wanted him just as much.

He took another step closer to the cliff. "You and me, Jeannie."

Small rocks shifted under my feet. They skittered over the side, down to the water far below.

"Not yet," I said. My heart was beating hard. "I've been saving all the money I can. Me and Charlie were going to run to the city. We can now, can't we? You're aboveground so—"

"The geas is broken." He nodded.

"Why don't you come with me, Robbie? Come to the city. We could be married for real. You could play. They'd pay you. You're the best fiddler I ever heard. You'd be rich!"

He kicked the ground, sending more dirt and rocks over the edge. "Under there, I *am* rich."

"Come with me, Robbie!" I tried to imagine him in a city, with tall buildings and cars and hardly any trees or flowers. I'd only ever seen him here. This small village, with its tiny green, its hill, its ash trees, the river. It was hard enough to imagine myself anywhere else.

He shook his head. "The city is steel and iron and chrome. It's cars and trucks and petrol, fumes and pollution. All of it burns. No, Jeannie, you have to come with me."

We were so close to the edge that even a slight tug and he'd send me over.

"I don't want to die."

"It's not death, Jeannie," he said, kissing my mouth. "It's a bigger life. A bigger world."

"I want a life with you, Robbie. I do. Far from my family and this village. But I want you to have a heart that beats. I want the Robbie that was before they came for you. Before you went underground. Please, Robbie, please come away with me."

He wrapped his arms around me tighter. I felt his kisses on the top of my head. My throat felt tight and my eyes burned with crying.

"I can't," he said. "When the sun sets, my clothes turn to feathers, my body to ash. In this world, I'm dead, Jeannie."

I squeezed him. Kissed his mouth again. His cheeks. His eyes. His neck. "But didn't you stop time?"

He laughed. "No. The sun's still moving and the ocean below. I might be fey, but I am not god."

"How long do we have?" I whispered. "An hour? Two?"

"An hour. At most."

We sank to the ground.

"Or you could come with me, Jeannie. It's beautiful there. . . ."

"What will your queen make of me? Won't they trick us apart? We can't trust them. Look how they turned you against me."

"But we won, Jeannie. They respect victors. You can learn to be a doctor there. It's a huge world. Vaster than this one."

"I don't believe in that world, Robbie. It's hard enough believing in the city."

"We'd be happy."

"And if I changed my mind? Would they let me return to this world?"

"You'd be fairy, Jeannie."

"Iron would burn me." I shook my head, unbuttoning his shirt. He pulled the jacket off, flung it away.

"I never forgot you."

He pulled my shirt over my head, kissed my belly. I felt the heat in my cheeks.

"You're still you, Robbie. Even without a heart."

"Yes."

We twined. We twisted. We covered every pore of our skin with kisses. Around us the world grew darker by the second.

"I have to go," he said, holding me tight. "Will you come?"

Part of me wanted to. I wanted to be with him forever. Past death, into his other world. But . . .

"I love you," I said. "I always will. No one but you."

"That's a promise?"

"Yes," I said and the word "promise" echoed inside me.

He kissed me again. Hard, pulling me closer to the edge. I felt him get heavier, felt his body slide toward the edge—toward the ocean and his green kingdom underneath. He was pulling me with him.

"Robbie, no," I said, fast as I could. "You promised me once. Remember? You said you'd never make me do anything I didn't want. I don't want this, Robbie."

He looked up at me. There were tears in his eyes. I had not known that fairy could cry.

"You promised."

"I love you," he said.

And then he let go. I fell back. He fell below.

"Goodbye, Robbie."

Beside me his clothes turned into feathers. The wind picked up, dragging them into the air and my hair all about me. I pushed back from the cliff, grabbing at my clothes before they were blown away, getting them back on me, and walking back into the village past the nosy tourists and their incessant cameras, past the narrow villagers who couldn't step away from the past.

Maggie ran up to chide me for leaving her daughter untended. I ignored her and picked up the jug and made my way back to Charlie's house.

A week later, we were in the city, living in a cheap boarding house. I found a bakery to work in, Charlie a newsagent's. They let us both back into school. In the city it was free.

The baby was born in May: Fay Greene. Both names for my Robbie.

# Fan Fictions

## GABRIELLE ZEVIN

# One

*Y*OU *KNOW* THIS GIRL.

Her hair is neither long nor short nor light nor dark. She parts it precisely in the middle.

She sits precisely in the middle of the classroom, and when she used to ride the school bus, she sat precisely in the middle of that, too.

She joins clubs, but is never the president of them. Sometimes she is the secretary; usually, just a member. When asked, she has been known to paint sets for the school play.

She always has a date to the dance, but is never anyone's first choice. In point of fact, she's nobody's first choice for anything. Her best friend became her best friend when another girl moved away.

She has a group of girls she eats lunch with every day,

but God, how they bore her. Sometimes, when she can't stand it anymore, she eats in the library instead. Truth be told, she prefers books to people, and the librarian always seems happy to see her.

She knows there are other people who have it worse—she isn't poor or ugly or friendless or teased. Of course, she's also aware that the reason no one teases is because no one ever notices her.

This isn't to say she doesn't have qualities.

She is pretty, maybe, if anyone would bother to look. And she gets good enough grades. And she doesn't drink and drive. And she says *NO* to drugs. And she is always where she says she will be. And she calls when she's going to be late. And she feels a little, *just a little*, dead inside.

She thinks, *You think you know me, but you don't.*

She thinks, *None of you has any idea about all the things in my heart.*

She thinks, *None of you has any idea how really and truly beautiful I am.*

She thinks, *See me. See me. See me.*

Sometimes she thinks she will scream.

Sometimes she imagines sticking her head in an oven.

But she doesn't.

She just writes it all down in her journal and waits.

She is waiting for someone to see.

# Two

THE SCHOOL LIBRARIAN IS new this year and she's barely older than the students. She wears tight pencil skirts and cashmere sweaters and patent leather Mary Janes. A librarian as styled by *Playboy*. Freshman boys have been known to invent special library errands just to look at her breasts. The new librarian is filled with ideas and book suggestions and what Paige—did I forget to mention the girl's name is Paige? No matter, it has happened before—what Paige considers an exhausting enthusiasm. Paige preferred the old librarian (who was also an *old* librarian), who had skin the same gray as the walls.

"Hi, Paige," the pinup librarian whispers conspiratorially. "You might like this one. It's new." She sets a book on the table in front of Paige. Its jacket is black and shiny.

No picture, just the title in silver: *The Immortals.*

Paige is doubtful. "What's it about?"

"It's a fantasy," says the librarian.

"The thing is, Ms. Penn, I sort of hate fantasy." Paige thinks that fantasy is for losers and people without real lives.

The librarian laughs. "It's a romance, too."

Paige thinks most modern romance is fluff, but she doesn't want to burst the pinup's bubble. "Well . . ."

The librarian laughs again. She's the type who's always laughing. "You don't have to marry it. Just give it a chance. If it's not your thing, just return it to the new release shelf on your way out."

Paige deigns to read the first paragraph:

*There are two kinds of people in the world: those who believe in love and those who don't. I believe in love.*

She closes the book. Indeed, it's not her thing. For one, Paige puts herself in the "nonbeliever" category.

She trudges over to the new books area to reshelve it. (The old librarian never would have made such a presumptuous request.) The author's last name starts with an R, and there's a convenient gap on the shelf awaiting *The Immortals*'s return.

Paige is about to take her hand off the shelf when she feels someone looking at her. She stays still for a moment, savoring the feeling of being seen. Finally, slowly, she turns.

She's definitely never seen (or been seen by) this boy before. His eyes are a hue she didn't know eyes came in— dark violet with flecks of silver and gray in the middle. He looks as if he could use a good night's sleep. His jacket is black and a little glossy, not unlike the book she's just returned to the shelf. There's something old-fashioned about him, but she can't quite place what it is. He is, for the record, distractingly handsome.

"Was it no good?" he asks.

"Someone thought I might like it, but it's not really my kind of story," she rambles. "I prefer old books. Classics, I guess."

"Too bad. I was hoping for a recommendation."

"*Wuthering Heights*," she suggests.

"I've already read it."

"*The Tin Drum.*"

Yes, he's read that, too. She names several other titles, and he's read all of them.

"Unless it's new," he says finally, "I've probably read it. I've read *everything.*"

*He's a liar,* she thinks. Or a braggart. Both probably. But the kind of a boy who bothers to brag (or lie) about being well-read piques her interest. "Are you new?" Paige asks.

The boy smiles, but it's not a happy one. "Oh, I suppose. This is about my millionth school." The bell rings, and he looks at her for a moment. "Shame you don't like new books, Paige. I was hoping I had found someone to talk to here." He looks her in the eyes, and for the first time in her life, Paige feels like someone is really and truly seeing her. "It can be lonely being the new kid in school." He says this last part really fast as if he'd rather not be saying it, but can't help himself.

And then he's gone.

Many moons later, when she is replaying this conversation for the millionth or so time in her head, she will wonder how he knew her name without even asking. But right now, what she thinks is, *It can be lonely being* any *kid in school.* She takes a pen from her pocket and writes "Everyone's lonely" on the palm of her hand. It's a revelation to her. She had thought she was the only one and had always taken pains to conceal her loneliness, the same way you'd hide a particularly gruesome scar.

She takes *The Immortals* off the shelf. She reads the first paragraph again:

*There are two kinds of people in the world: those who believe in love and those who don't. I believe in love.*

Somehow, it seems different, better, even good this time.

# Three

THAT NIGHT IN BED, she tries to study but can't concentrate.

She picks up her library book, but that's no good, either. It just reminds her of strange violet eyes.

She doesn't particularly like thinking about him or anyone else. Most people tend to be disappointing once you actually get to know them, and she has been disappointed by so many before.

She knows nothing much happened between them; nothing important was said.

And yet . . .

She tosses the book aside.

She looks at herself in the mirror and wonders if she looks different than she did that morning.

Her father knocks on the door: Paige's mother is on

the phone and would like to speak to her.

"I'm reading," Paige says. "I'll call her back."

Paige decides that she *is* different. From now on, she will part her hair on the left side.

# Four

SHE IS DIFFERENT, WHICH means she doesn't do the things she'd normally do in a situation like this.

She doesn't go back to the library the next day to try to find him.

She decides to take it slow. It's like reading a really good book—a pretty good book you want to rush through, but a really good book you want to read slowly, delaying the moment when you will reach that last page, sentence, word as long as possible. She believes . . . no, she *knows* she will see him again. Or he will see her. She just has to be patient.

She doesn't ask her friends about the "new boy," either. If she talks about him, the others will try to track him down and then he won't be hers anymore. She doesn't want to share. She wants him to be her secret.

*It's lovely to have a secret,* she thinks.

At lunch, Polly, the one she calls her best friend, says to Paige, "You seem different."

"It's her hair," another girl says. "She's parting it on the left."

*It's lovely to have a secret,* Paige thinks.

# Five

HE MANAGES TO WAIT three more days before
returning to the library.

Ms. Penn hands Paige a flyer as she is walking past the
checkout desk. "I'm starting an all-girl's book club," she
says. "Get your friends to come, okay, Paige?"

Paige nods. She wants to ask Ms. Penn if he's here in
the library, but then Paige remembers that she doesn't
even know his name.

"The first book's gonna be that one I told you about,
*The Immortals*. I thought it'd be fun to start with something new. Now I know you aren't a 'fantasy' girl, but I'm
telling you, Paige, I read it over the weekend and I didn't
even want to stop to eat. I read it while I was driving. It's
that good. And you're going to love the boy in it—"

"Ms. Penn, I really have to go."

"Oh, okay, take a bunch of flyers to pass out, would you?"

Paige stuffs the flyers in her bag and walks to the new books row. All of a sudden, she feels nervous. What if he isn't there? Or what if he *is* there and he doesn't even remember who she is? It would almost be worse to be forgotten by him than to never see him again. And why had she even thought he'd come back there in the first place? And why had she waited three days and given him all that time to disappear? And why hadn't she given him her number that first day?

Aside from books, the row is empty when she gets there. She crouches down and pretends to be considering a novel on the bottom shelf. But really what she's doing is crying.

*I'm an idiot,* she thinks.

*You didn't even know this boy's name,* she thinks.

And then, there's a hand on her shoulder.

"I'd almost given up hope," he says. "I've been here every day since we met."

She turns and, if anything, he is more handsome than she remembered. Paige bites her lip to stop from giggling—his looks are ridiculous really, like something out of a storybook.

He offers his hand to help her up. "My name's Aaron."

They talk for the rest of lunch. At first, it's just about books, but it expands to other things, too. She finds herself telling him things she has never told anyone. She even talks about her mother. "She left my dad last year. She says she fell in love with someone else, but I don't believe it. I think she just fell out of love with my dad. I think it's sort of messed me up for relationships actually."

He laughs. "Everyone's messed up."

"Are you?"

"Yeah, pretty much. I've vowed not to have any more relationships, if you want to know the truth."

She wonders what his story is.

She wonders what he's doing with her.

And without her even having to ask, he tells her, "I'm here because you're the most interesting person in this whole damn place.

"I'm here because, despite everything, I still believe," he says.

He doesn't say *what* he still believes, and she doesn't ask.

The bell rings, and Paige stands instinctively—a Pavlovian good girl to her very core.

"I bet if we stay real quiet, no one will even notice us here," he says.

Paige thinks, *He's right. No one's ever noticed me before.*

He reads her mind. "They just weren't looking close enough."

"Am I so easy for you to read?" she asks, a bit embarrassed.

"Yes, but only because I'm really paying attention."

The warning bell rings, but this time she sits back down among Aaron and the books.

"I'm glad you came here," Paige says.

"I'm glad I did, too."

He takes her hand in his. What she had written on her palm is almost completely faded away.

They hide out in the library for the rest of the day, even though Paige is most definitely not the kind of girl to skip. Ms. Penn doesn't notice them, or at least, that's what Ms. Penn pretends. Ms. Penn, you see, likes Paige. She likes Paige because she's been Paige. She used to part her hair in the middle, too.

Without really knowing how they got there, they end up at her house after school.

In her room.

The first thing he does is go over to her bookshelf where he considers all her titles. "You really are a reader," he says, pleased. Paige blushes—reading has never gotten her anything in life except, maybe, personal enjoyment. It has certainly never gotten her a boyfriend.

"I sometimes prefer books to people," she admits.

"Me, too," he says.

When her dad gets home from work, Paige asks Aaron if he wants to meet her father.

Aaron shakes his head. "Some other time. I'm not that good with families. My own or other people's." And then, he slips out her window with a wink that Paige wishes was something else.

# Six

IT'S NOT PERFECT.

For one, there are things he doesn't talk about.

His family.

His past.

Why he left those other schools.

Other places he's lived.

Other girls he's loved.

And then, there are all the things about him that don't add up.

He's seventeen, a senior, a reader, but has no plans to go to college.

He never eats.

He's absent from school more than he's there.

She's never seen his house.

And of course, she's never met anyone in his family.

*But everyone has problems,* Paige thinks. No one is perfect, and what she knows for certain is that he is beautiful and he makes her feel beautiful. And when she talks, he really listens. And when he looks at her, he sees. And—

Paige is in her science class when someone taps her on the shoulder. "You haven't been at lunch in ages," says April, one of Paige's lunchtime friends. "What happened?"

"I was in the library. I'm helping with this book club thing," Paige lies. She doesn't know why she lied. She did it without even thinking. She grabs one of those crumpled book club flyers that have been cluttering the bottom of her bag for about two weeks—has it really only been two weeks since she met him? She feels like she's known him forever—and gives it to April.

"Cool," says April without even looking at it. "Ms. Penn already gave me one. The thing is, I needed to talk to you about something. You know how Homecoming's next month?"

Paige had forgotten. She's been distracted for obvious reasons. "Uh, yeah."

"My brother wanted to know if you'd go with him."

April's brother is, for lack of a better word, a nerd. For one, he's a grade below Paige. For two, he's kind of overweight. For three, he's very into role-playing games. Paige suspects he'd probably want to play them with her at the dance. Paige laughs at the thought.

"Why are you laughing?" April asks. "It's mean of you to laugh."

Paige doesn't want to be mean. "I'm sorry. I was thinking of something else. . . . Honestly. Something funny that happened earlier."

"What was it?" April looks at Paige with hard eyes.

"It was this joke. It was this thing. It was . . . It was . . ." Paige can't come up with anything funny that doesn't involve role-playing, so she returns to the subject at hand. "The point is, I'm not laughing at your brother. It's just . . . if he wanted to go with me why didn't he ask me himself?"

April's eyes soften. For the moment, Paige has pacified her. "He's shy, Paige! You know that! So, will you go with him?"

"I'm kind of seeing someone," Paige says.

"You never mentioned anyone before," April says coldly.

"It's early."

"So, will *he* be taking you to Homecoming?"

"We haven't talked about it yet," Paige admits.

"It can't be that serious if you haven't talked about it."

Paige doesn't answer. She knows what she has with Aaron and she doesn't care what anyone thinks.

"Well, don't mention this to anyone, okay?" says April. "You weren't my brother's first choice anyway. I was the one who told him to ask you. I thought you'd say yes."

Despite the fact that Paige keeps her promise and tells no one about the embarrassing incident with April's brother (*as if she would!*), April tells everyone that Paige is seeing someone. And that night, Paige gets a call from Polly. "When are we going to meet him?" Polly demands.

"It's early," Paige repeats. "We're not quite there." Paige promises that when the time is right, the best friend will be the first.

"Just give me a little something to tide me over, okay?" Polly insists. "Just tell me his name. You don't even have to say the last. Just the first."

"Aaron," Paige says hoarsely.

"Does he go here?"

Paige says that she isn't ready to talk about him yet.

"You've got to ask him to Homecoming, Paige! We can all go together—me and Luke, and you and Aaron."

Paige hates even hearing the best friend say his name. "It's not like that," she says. "He's not like other boys."

"*Gawd*, Paige, this sounds serious."

Paige concedes that yes, it, sort of, is.

Even though she knows she probably shouldn't, Paige broaches the subject of Homecoming with him that night in her room. "I know it's kind of lame, but do you think you might want to go?"

He doesn't. He says he's been to a hundred Home-coming dances before.

"Oh." Paige tries to mask her disappointment by silently reading titles from her bookshelf—*Wuthering Heights, Jane Eyre, Frankenstein . . .*

"Why do you need some stupid dance anyway? Don't you know what you are to me?"

In point of fact, Paige doesn't. In point of fact, Paige would very much like to be seen at the dance with some-one as handsome as Aaron. Let's just say that she has spent more than her share of dances with people's broth-ers and the equivalent.

"Look, Paige," he says, "I want us to be together, but I can't do the things that other boyfriends can."

It is the first time he has called himself that—her boyfriend. She wishes it had been some other time, the way it would have happened in the kind of books Paige claims not to read.

"Do you understand?" he asks.

Paige says she does, but she doesn't really. "Do you . . . do you have another girlfriend or something?" She stumbles a bit over the word *girlfriend*: the lovely new-ness of it.

Aaron sighs. He takes her hands in his. "Of course not."

She pulls away from him. "You don't tell me anything about yourself really."

"I want to tell you everything, but I can't. . . . It could hurt people other than myself."

"Your family?"

He nods. "If I tell you and you tell anyone, I'll have to leave here. As much as it will kill me, I'll leave and I won't even be able to say goodbye."

"You can trust me," she says.

"I . . . I really don't like to talk about these things."

"You don't have to, then," she says. "But I just want you to know that you can trust me."

He looks at her and nods slowly. "I think maybe I can."

Paige's father calls from downstairs. "Dinner!"

"I should go anyway," Aaron says.

Paige doesn't know if he means permanently or just for a couple of hours. She grabs his hands. They are dry, almost papery. "Promise me you'll come back. I want so much to know your story. I want to know everything about you."

"I'll try." He slips out of Paige's house through the window.

"Dinner!" Paige's father calls again.

"Coming," Paige says.

Paige goes downstairs to the kitchen. They are eating macaroni and cheese, which means it's Tuesday. Paige's father has a dish for each of the six days of the week. On Sundays, he orders pizza.

"I've been calling you for about ten minutes. Didn't you hear me?" Paige's father asks.

"Just reading," Paige says absently.

"Must be *some* book," her father comments.

As soon as dinner is over, Paige rushes back up to her room, but Aaron isn't there. She busies herself for several hours with the schoolwork she's been neglecting, but he still doesn't come. Eventually, she decides to curl up with a novel in bed, but before she's even read a chapter, she falls asleep.

She is still sleeping when she becomes aware of someone whispering in her ear.

She reaches for the light, which her father must have turned off.

"No," Aaron says, "some stories are easier told in the dark."

When he was seventeen, there was a tuberculosis outbreak in his town. His father was the first to get it, and fewer than six weeks later, his father was the first to die.

Despite herself, Paige wonders, *People still die of TB?*

His whole family—Aaron, his sister, and his mother—got TB, too. "I honestly can't describe it," he says. "It was horrible. To see someone you love die slowly and painfully, and then to know that soon, you will die the same way."

His sister died about a week after his father. And he

and his mother knew that it wouldn't be long for them, either. "There's a strange sort of quiet when you're dying," he says. "It's as if you're in a glass room, and the walls keep getting thicker and thicker."

Paige tries to take his hand. She wants to touch him, to comfort him. Between her drowsiness and the low light, though, she can't quite find him.

Lacking other options, his mother went to see a gypsy in town.

*A gypsy? Where in the world was this town? Medieval Europe?* "A gypsy?" Paige asks softly.

"My mother did the best she could," Aaron says. "It was a different place. A different time."

The gypsy gave her a peacock-blue glass jar shaped like an inkwell. She claimed that inside was an elixir from a spring in Mexico and that it would heal them. What choice did they have? They crossed themselves and drank deeply. "Our lungs cleared instantly," he says. "The glass walls were shattered."

But it didn't just heal them.

They have lived in fifty different towns. His mother has been married twelve times. She gets a new husband every time the old one starts to suspect. Aaron has had girlfriends. "Many," he says, which makes Paige cringe. Aaron has had many girlfriends, but they all eventually outgrow him. He was born in 1876. He will be seventeen years old for the rest of his life.

Paige tells him that she doesn't believe in fantasy stories, that if he didn't want to go to Homecoming with her, he should have just said so.

"I would never lie to you." He finds her hand now. Her eyes are growing more accustomed to the moonlight. He helps her out of bed and moves her so that they are standing side by side in front of her bedroom mirror.

"Do you see?"

She shakes her head. She doesn't know what she's supposed to be seeing and besides, she hasn't taken her eyes off him.

"Look in the mirror. I don't have a reflection. I'm not there."

She obeys. Her eyes move from the mirror to him and back again. She runs her hand in front of his face. Her hand is reflected. His face is not. It frightens her: She looks like she is alone. She looks lonely, and this is something Paige tries never to look.

"Why?" she asks.

"I don't know. It's just the way it is, the way I am." He tries to turn it into a sort of a joke. "Makes it a bit hard getting ready in the mornings, but I do my best."

Then, he takes a Swiss Army knife out of his pocket.

"What's the knife for?" Paige squeaks. Her throat always constricts when she is panicking.

Aaron flips the knife open and moves the blade toward his arm. He punctures his flesh with the blade. For a second,

Paige is paralyzed and can do nothing but stare.

He carves a J into his arm.

"Don't!" Paige finds her voice. "Please don't! I believe you. You don't have to prove anything to me." She tries to stop him, in case the J is merely the beginning of a longer word like "Jealousy" or "Jilted," but he holds her back.

"Why would you do that to yourself?" Paige whimpers.

A second later, the cut begins to heal before her eyes. She runs her fingers along his cold, perfect arm, and then she presses her lips to it.

"I want you to go to your dance, but I can't be there with you," he says. "I've been to too many before."

*But never with me,* she thinks.

"You're different," he says, "but the dances . . . they're always the same."

She nods. She's a bit disappointed, but still happy to have been trusted with his story.

"I really love you," he says.

"I really love you, too."

They lie down in her bed and after a while, she falls back asleep. When she wakes in the morning, he's gone. If she weren't so exhausted, she'd probably think the whole night had been a dream.

Paige considers not going to the dance at all, but Aaron convinces her to go. "You only have Homecoming once," he says.

"Not true in your case," she points out. "Or mine. They're every year, you know."

He laughs a little. "Go," he says. "I don't want you to miss things because of me."

The truth is she's more than willing to miss things because of him, but she can't say that. It would sound needy, clingy, pathetic. Paige hates people like that. "You could still come," Paige reminds him instead.

Aaron just shakes his head.

Paige's father knocks on the door while she is getting ready. "Come in," Paige says. Aaron hides behind the side of her bookshelf—Paige isn't supposed to have boys in her bedroom.

"You look really beautiful," her father says. "Who's the lucky guy?"

"No one," Paige says, standing up from her vanity. "The boy I wanted to go with couldn't come, and I wouldn't settle for anyone else." She winks at Aaron in the mirror. She can't see him, but she imagines he can see her.

The dance is a dance, which is to say, it's like every other dance Paige has ever been to—more fun in theory than in execution. Paige's feet hurt from her shoes, and she wishes she had just spent the night at home curled up with Aaron after all.

Toward the end of the evening, Paige runs into April.

"What happened to your boyfriend?"

"He couldn't come."

"Guess you should have gone with my brother, then."

Paige narrows her eyes. She knows she shouldn't say anything to April, but she can't help herself. "Honestly, April, that was never going to happen, so stop embarrassing both of us by bringing it up."

When Paige gets home that night, Aaron is waiting for her in her bedroom. He's wearing a tuxedo. He looks so handsome, she almost wants to die. "I thought we could have our own Homecoming right here," he says.

He kisses her and pulls her close to him. Her body trembles.

"Sometimes it's hard to believe you're real," she says. "Sometimes it's hard to believe you're mine."

"I think the same thing," he says.

"No. I mean, really. You're just so perfect."

Aaron shakes his head. "I'm not. Trust me, I'm not."

Paige looks over Aaron's shoulder and sees what should be hers and Aaron's reflection in the bedroom mirror.

The sight disturbs her. Aaron, of course, has no reflection, and it looks as if her arms are wrapped around air.

# Seven

"APRIL THINKS YOU DON'T really have a boyfriend," Polly reports to Paige the Monday after the dance. Aaron is absent that day, so Paige is giving Polly a ride home.

Paige laughs. "She's just pissed because I wouldn't go to the dance with her freak brother."

Polly laughs, too. "But seriously, Paige, you're being so secretive about this whole thing. Why is it all such a secret?"

"It just is."

Polly shakes her head. "My older sister had a boyfriend like this once."

"Like what?"

"Like not wanting to meet her friends or ever take her out in public and stuff like that. And it turned out he was hurting her."

"Aaron's not like that."

"Neither was my sister's boyfriend at first!"

"Listen, Polly, you don't know what you're even talking about."

"Then make me understand. Honestly, I'm worried about you."

It's an odd thing, but Polly's concern is sort of flattering to Paige. No one's been that interested in her in years. And she has been dying to talk about Aaron with someone. So, she swears Polly to secrecy and tells his story.

Polly is quiet for a long time, and then she does something horrible: she laughs. "Oh, Paige," she says, "I think he's playing with you!"

"What do you mean?"

"I mean, seriously! Seriously! A gypsy? It sounds like something from a book. I think he's telling you a story. He probably tells this to every girl he meets. I think he's just—"

"SHUT UP! You don't know anything about it. About him. You just don't want me to be happy!"

"Paige, don't be hurt—"

Paige stops the car several blocks from Polly's house. "Get out."

By the time she pulls into her driveway, Paige's hands are shaking and she's out of breath. She needs to see Aaron and touch him, remind herself that he's real.

When she gets into her house, he is waiting for her in her bedroom. He had let himself in through her window.

"What is it?" he asks.

"I had a fight with my friend."

"I'm sorry," he says, stroking her hair.

"Why weren't you in school today?" Paige asks.

"My mother's sick."

"I thought your kind couldn't get sick."

"Physically, yes," he says with a tired sigh. "Mentally, though . . ."

"I wish I could help you," Paige says.

"You *are* helping me."

Paige looks into his violet-silver eyes. She decides that she doesn't care if he is lying to her. It's a beautiful lie. He's a beautiful lie.

That night, Paige has a nightmare:

She is in the school library. She is standing in the new books row. And across the room, she sees someone kissing Aaron—it's Ms. Penn! And then, Polly is kissing him, too. And then April is taking off his shirt. And then all the girls she eats lunch with have their hands all over him. Even Paige's own mother is kissing Aaron, as disgusting as that sounds. Paige calls his name, but he doesn't seem to hear her at first. He turns to the side to see who is calling him and that's when she realizes it isn't Aaron at all. It's just a cardboard cutout version of him. It's flat and shiny: a life-size paper doll.

# Eight

*T*HE NEXT DAY AT school, everywhere she goes, she's not sure, but she thinks she hears people (and especially girls) talking about Aaron and looking at her. She only catches every other word or so, but what she hears sounds something like this: new boy . . . library . . . Aaron . . . immortal . . . page . . .

Paige can barely breathe or walk or speak. It can only be one thing: Polly has told everyone their story, his secret. She doesn't want to contemplate what this might mean.

She goes to find him in their usual spot in the library. He's not there, but Ms. Penn is.

"Don't forget about the book club tomorrow. I know for a fact lots of people are coming, and you still have time to finish *The Im*—"

"I don't give a crap about your stupid book club!"

"Paige, is something wrong?"

Paige pushes past Ms. Penn and runs out of the library.

She sneaks out of school and drives back to her house. She hopes that he will be in her room waiting for her, but he's not.

Paige gets down on her knees and prays. "Please God let me see him. . . . Please God let me see him. . . . Please God let me see him. . . ."

She knows she doesn't deserve him (maybe she never did), but she wants to apologize at least.

# Nine

$\mathcal{P}$AIGE HASN'T SLEPT AT all. She shouldn't go to school, but she does on the off chance that he might be there.

At lunch, she goes to the library to look for him. The place is unusually noisy and crowded. *Oh, right,* Paige thinks. *Ms. Penn's crappy book club.* She spots Polly, April, and all the girls from their lunch table. Seeing them sitting there makes Paige momentarily forget Aaron. Seeing them with those stupid black books on their stupid skinny laps stirs something almost violent in her. She hates seeing them in the library. What a joke! Like any of them even read anything that's not for school! The library is *her place.* And she hates slutty Ms. Penn with her slutty tight sweaters for actually going out of the way to coax these jerks here.

Ms. Penn waves Paige over as if nothing had happened between them yesterday. "Paige, I'm *so* glad you came...."

Paige tells Ms. Penn that she isn't there for the book club, but rather, to meet someone. "I'm sorry. I'll try to make it to the end, if I can," Paige says. Out of the corner of her eye, she sees April whispering to Polly. She doesn't have to hear to know that they are talking about her and Aaron.

Paige walks to the new books row. It's empty just like it had been the day before.

She rests her hand on the shelf where she had returned *The Immortals* that first day she met him. Somehow, she believes that if she does the same things from the day she met him, she might just be able to conjure him again. But it doesn't work. She can't do the same things anyway, as the library's copy of that particular book has been checked out.

Paige sinks to the ground and rests her head on her knees.

The only sound in the library is Ms. Penn's book club, of course.

She wishes they would leave.

She tries to tune them out, but it's impossible. They're so damn noisy.

"Oh, I know," she hears one of them saying, "the saddest part was when he was telling about his father getting pneumonia."

"No, the saddest part was when he had to leave because everyone knew his secret," another chimes in.

"No, the saddest part was how lonely she was after he left. . . ."

"Yeah, but didn't you think she was kind of pathetic actually? I mean, why would he have even picked someone like her? No one even notices her."

"That's the point, I think. . . ."

Paige can barely breathe; her pulse races; she feels as if her heart might break. Or stop beating. The nerve of these girls—they're not even discussing the book. They're just gossiping about her!

Paige rises from the ground and runs back to where the book club is meeting.

Ms. Penn sees her first. "Paige, join us," she says.

"STOP TALKING ABOUT ME!" Paige yells.

A few of the girls laugh.

Ms. Penn clears her throat. She stands. "No one was talking about you, Paige."

"Yes, you were! I heard you! I'm not deaf!"

Ms. Penn walks over to Paige. "No, we weren't. We were just talking about the book." She holds out the library's copy of *The Immortals* for Paige to see. "We were just talking about the merits of the main character, Aaron."

Paige looks around the book club circle. All the girls stare back at her.

Finally, Polly speaks. "I think Paige misunderstood

'cause her boyfriend's name is also Aaron."

"Oh . . ." says Ms. Penn, and then she laughs, relieved. "That makes sense!" she says. "Of course, I highly doubt your Aaron is a violet-gray-eyed, hundred-fifty-year-old in a seventeen-year-old's body, right, Paige?"

The girls laugh their hyena laughs.

"Stop," Paige whispers.

But no one seems to hear.

"STOP!"

No one *ever* hears.

"STOP MAKING FUN OF ME!"

They are silent. They are scared. Paige has just crossed the line from amusing freak to could-possibly-have-a-gun, and she doesn't even care.

Polly speaks softly. "Wait, I get it. I think I . . . I only started reading the night before and I'm not quite done— sorry, Ms. Penn—but I think I just put it together. That guy you were seeing . . . He borrowed his story from this book, didn't he?"

"No," Paige says. "No, he would never do that!"

"Yes, he did. I'm sure of it. He even used the name!"

"SHUT UP SHUT UP SHUT UP! You're the reason he's gone in the first place!"

Polly says she doesn't know what Paige is talking about.

"Liar! I know you told everyone! You and your big dumb mouth!"

"Paige," Polly says. "Calm down. I didn't. I swear I didn't."

Ms. Penn is still holding out the book to Paige. Without thinking, Paige grabs the book from her. Ms. Penn topples backward. Maybe Ms. Penn bangs her head on the chair behind her? Maybe she catches herself? Paige doesn't know. She doesn't wait to find out. She runs out, clutching the library's copy of *The Immortals* to her breast.

She makes it to her car. Luckily, the school parking lot gate is still unlocked for the seniors who leave school at lunch.

She doesn't go home. She doesn't know if she's in trouble or not. She just drives and drives and thinks and thinks.

*Is it possible that Polly is right and Aaron borrowed his story from the book?*

She drives and drives . . .

*No, it can't be.*

Eventually, she decides to park in a movie theater parking lot the next town over.

*But what if . . . ?*

She takes the copy of *The Immortals* from the passenger seat and begins to read.

# Ten

OU KNOW THIS STORY.

She reads the cover: *The Immortals* by Anna-belle Reve.

She turns to the first page.

*"There are two kinds of people in the world: those who believe in love and those who don't. I believe in love. . . ."*

She's flipping pages so quickly she gets a paper cut.

*". . . lonely being the new kid in school . . ."*

*". . . because you're the most interesting person in the whole damn place . . ."*

*"They just weren't looking close enough."*

*"As much as it will kill me, I'll leave, Jane, and I won't even be able to say goodbye."*

Paige can't even finish reading the book. What she feels is violated. It's as if someone has been wiretapping every single conversation she has ever had with Aaron and then transcribed them for all the world to see. *To read!* Even their most private exchanges. Things that no one in the world could have known. The only real change is Paige's name. In the book, Paige is called Jane. Reading that name feels like being burned. Or erased.

She turns to the back jacket flap. "Annabelle Reve," she reads, "lives in New York City with her son. *The Immortals* is her first novel." There's a color photograph of her, too. She looks to be in her early thirties. *She's pretty,* Paige decides. *Like someone from an old painting.* And then, Paige notices Annabelle Reve's eyes—they're gray and violet just like . . .

Paige rereads the bio. No mention of a husband. *Just a son.*

It doesn't necessarily add up, but Paige does know one thing: She has to find Annabelle Reve.

Paige calls Information on the off chance that Annabelle Reve is listed; she is. No phone number, but there is an address and it's not even that far from where Paige lives. Paige calculates that it will only take about forty minutes to get there, if traffic is good.

# *Eleven*

W HEN PAIGE WAS A little girl, her mother used to
let her skip school to see the Wednesday mati-
nees on Broadway. This is to say she has visited New York
City many times and she locates Annabelle Reve's apartment building without any problem.

It's a nice, old building with an impressive lobby and,
unfortunately for Paige, a doorman.

"I'm here to see Annabelle Reve," Paige says as confi-
dently as possible.

The doorman informs Paige that Ms. Reve isn't
home.

"Um . . . Maybe I could just wait in her place until
she's back. I'm her niece. She's my aunt. She's expecting
me," Paige lies easily. "I'm visiting from out of town."

"Listen, kid, I'd like to help," the doorman says not

unkindly. "But Ms. Reve didn't say anything about a niece visiting. You can wait down here, but that's the best I can do."

So Paige sits on the green velvet couch in the lobby and waits. It isn't that long before she falls asleep.

When she wakes, Annabelle Reve is looking at her with those familiar violet-gray eyes.

"They told me my niece was waiting for me in the lobby. I suppose you would be her." Annabelle has a half smile on her face. She offers Paige her hand to shake. "Annabelle."

"Paige."

"Would you like to come upstairs for a bit?"

Paige nods and follows Annabelle into the elevator.

In the apartment, Annabelle puts a kettle on the stove.

"I've had letters and emails, of course, but you're the first to show up here," Annabelle calls from the kitchen. "The book's only been out a month, so it's looking like I'm going to have to become unlisted, I guess."

Paige doesn't say anything.

"That's why you're here, right?" Annabelle asks. "*The Immortals.*"

"Yes."

"So, you've come all this way . . . Where'd you say you were from again?"

"New Jersey," Paige says. She thinks to herself, *I know*

*you know where I'm from. You know everything about me. Aaron told you everything about me.*

"Well, not too far, then, but still a lot of effort. So, what do you want to know?"

Paige has so many questions, but she can only manage one. "Is Aaron here?"

Annabelle emerges from the kitchen carrying a tray with a teapot and two cups. "Come again?"

"I want to know if Aaron is here."

Annabelle nods and pours Paige a cup of tea. "Well, if you mean the character Aaron, I suppose, in a way, he's here in that he's inside my head, and I did write the entire book inside this apartment.

"And if you mean, my son, Aaron? I really don't know why you would want to know about that, but he's staying with his father this week."

"I thought Aaron's father was dead," Paige says.

"Well, in the story, yes. In real life, we're just divorced. I guess I thought I was being clever. My ex-husband, probably not so much."

"But . . . but . . . the rest is all real?" Paige stammers. "I mean, Aaron is a real person. I mean, I *know* him."

"Paige . . ." Annabelle looks into Paige's eyes. Those eyes are so like Aaron's that Paige nearly wants to cry for missing him. "The Aaron in the book isn't a real person, but I did name him for a real person. My son. He's four years old." Annabelle laughs sweetly. "He's probably gonna kill me for doing that when he gets older."

"You're lying. You have to be lying." Paige stands and begins to pace Annabelle Reve's bookshelf-lined living room. "Because if you're not lying, how did you find out all that stuff about me, then? How were you able to put my whole life into that book?"

Annabelle walks over to Paige and takes her hand. "I'm flattered that the characters in my story were so . . . um . . . vivid to you. But I think you've made a mistake."

"LET GO OF ME! JUST TELL ME WHERE AARON IS!" Paige screams. "I KNOW YOU HAVE HIM SOME-WHERE. HE TALKED ABOUT YOU. HE TALKED ABOUT HIS CRAZY MOTHER WHO'S ALWAYS MAKING HIM MOVE!"

"I . . ."

Paige begins to cry. "I know I screwed up. I know I'm bad. But I love him. And I can't live without him. Please don't keep him from me. I love him. I believe in love." Paige sits on the floor. She puts her hands around her knees and rocks herself. "I believe in love," she whimpers. "I believe in love. I believe in love. . . ."

Annabelle excuses herself. She goes into her bedroom where she calls the doorman first and, then, the police.

# Twelve

FOR THE WHOLE FIRST week she's there, they won't even let her have a pencil, and she feels like she might really go crazy. Things that happen to her don't seem real until she can write them down. And of course, she wants to write Aaron even though she's not supposed to contact him anymore, even though she's not exactly sure where he is.

The doctor asks if she knows why she's there, and she replies, "Because my parents don't like my boyfriend, and they're trying to keep us apart."

The doctor nods, but doesn't say anything.

"They're cynical," Paige says. "You know they're divorced, right?"

"I think you may have mentioned it before."

"The point is . . . My point is . . . they're both so

bitter it's disgusting."

"It sounds sad, actually."

"It *is* sad. . . . But I'm not like them. I will *never* be like them." She lowers her voice, "I'm here because you think I'm crazy. But everyone who's ever loved anyone is crazy, right? So that makes me normal. And do you know what I think is really, really crazy?"

"No."

"What's really and truly crazy is not to love at all."

The doctor nods, but it is unclear if she agrees.

"I want to show you something," the doctor says. She takes a copy of *The Immortals* out from her desk.

When Paige sees it, she begins to drum her fingers on the table.

"Does the book make you nervous?"

Paige doesn't speak.

"You contend," the doctor continues, "that the author Annabelle Reve stole your story, the details of your relationship with her son, Aaron, and turned it into her novel?"

Paige nods.

"Well, what if I told you that Annabelle Reve had written the whole book before you even met Aaron? Would that change things for you?"

Paige doesn't answer.

"And what if I told you that the librarian at your school saw you reading this book?"

"That woman's a whore," Paige says. "You should see how she dresses."

"So she's lying about having seen you read this book?"

Paige doesn't answer.

"Have you ever heard of Occam's razor?"

"Yes," Paige says. "We studied that in science. It's the theory that the simplest solution is usually the correct one."

"Good. So you tell me which is more likely: Annabelle Reve stole your story and is now hiding your immortal boyfriend, that no one—not your parents, not your friends—ever saw, *or* that you read a book by Annabelle Reve and identified with it so closely that you somehow made the story your own?"

"I know what I know," Paige says. "All anyone knows is what they know. All we know is what we know, doctor."

Paige walks across the room. She picks up the copy of *The Immortals* and then she throws it at the doctor as hard as she can. "All I know is that love is crazy," Paige says.

It is several more weeks before they allow Paige a pencil.

"*Dear Aaron, There's . . .*" she writes and then she crumples up the piece of paper. She's not supposed to contact him anymore, and she doesn't know when she'll be able to send this, or where. She worries all the time that maybe he's been trying to contact her. And there's no privacy here. They search her things all the time. It's to help with her recovery, they say. It's to keep her safe. So she'll just have to imagine his name at the top of the page and know in her heart, where everything is still true and clear and pure, that she's writing him.

Writing *to* him, that is.

She takes out a blank piece of paper.

"Dear Aaron," she whispers to herself, and then she writes, *"There are two kinds of people in this world: those who don't believe in love and those who do. I believe in love...."*

*Love Struck*

MELISSA MARR

ESPITE IT BEING AT the beach, the party was lame. A few people were trying to turn noise into music: if Alana had been high or drunk, it might've been tolerable. But she was sober—and tense. Usually, the beach was where she found peace and pleasure; it was one of the only places where she felt like the world wasn't impossibly out of order. But tonight, she felt anxious.

A guy sat down beside her; he held out a cup. "You look thirsty."

"I'm not thirsty"—she glanced at him and tore her gaze away as quickly as she could—"*or* interested." *Eye candy.* She didn't date eye candy. She'd been watching her mother do that for years. It was so not the path Alana was taking. *Ever.* Instead, she stared at the singer.

He was normal, not-tempting, not-exciting. He was cute and sweet, but not irresistible. That was the sort of guy Alana chose when she dated—safe, temporary, and easy to leave.

She smiled at the singer. The bad rendition of a Beatles song shifted into a worse attempt at poetry . . . or maybe a cover of something new and emo. It didn't really matter what it was: Alana was going to listen to it and not pay attention to the hot dreadlocked guy who was sitting too close beside her.

Dreadlocks, however, wasn't taking the hint.

"Are you cold? Here." He tossed a long brown leather coat on the sand in front of her. It looked completely out of place for the crowd at the party.

"No, thanks." Alana scooted a bit away from him, closer to the fire. Burnt embers swirled and lifted like fireflies rising with the smoke.

"You'll get cold walking home and—"

"Go away. Please." Alana still didn't look back at him. Polite wasn't working. "I'm not interested, easy, or going to get drunk enough to be either of those. Seriously."

He laughed, seeming not insulted but genuinely amused. "Are you *sure*?"

"Leave."

"It'd be easier this way. . . ."

He moved closer, putting himself between her and the fire, directly in her line of view.

And she had to look, not a quick glance, but a real look. Illuminated by the combined glow of firelight and moonlight, he was even more stunning than she'd feared: blond hair clumped in thick dreadlocks that stretched to his waist; a few of those thick strands were kelp-green; his tattered T-shirt had holes that allowed glimpses of the most defined abs she'd ever seen.

He was crouched down, balancing on his feet. "Even if it wouldn't upset Murrin, it'd be tempting to take you."

Dreadlocks reached out as if he was going to cup her face in his hand.

Alana crab-walked backward, scuttling over the sand until she was just out of his reach. She scrambled to her feet and slipped a hand into the depths of her bag, past her shoes and her jumble of keys. She gripped her pepper spray and flicked the safety switch off, but didn't pull it out of her bag yet. Logic said she was overreacting: There were other people around; she was safe here. But something about him felt wrong.

"Back off," she said.

He didn't move. "Are you sure? Really, it'd be easier for you this way. . . ."

She pulled out the pepper spray.

"It's your choice, precious. It'll be worse once he finds you." Dreadlocks paused as if she'd say something or change her mind.

She'd couldn't reply to comments that made no

sense, though—and she surely wasn't going to change her mind about getting closer to him.

He sighed. "I'll be back after he breaks you."

Then he walked away, heading toward the mostly empty parking lot.

She watched until she was sure he was gone. Grappling with drunk or high or whatever-he-was guys wasn't on her to do list. She'd taken self-defense and street-defense classes, heard countless lectures on safety, and kept her pepper spray handy—her mother was very good about *that* part of parenting. None of that meant she wanted to have to use those lessons.

She looked around the beach. There were some strangers at the party, but mostly the people there were ones she'd seen around at school or out walking the reef. Right now, none of them was paying any attention to her. No one even looked her way. Some had watched when she was backing away from Dreadlocks, but they'd stopped watching when he left.

Alana couldn't decide if he was just messing with her or if someone there really posed a threat . . . or if he was saying that to spook her into leaving the party so she'd be alone and vulnerable. Usually, when she walked home, she went in the same direction he'd gone, but just in case he was lurking in the parking lot, she decided to go farther down the beach and cut across Coast Highway. It was a couple blocks out of the way, but he'd creeped her out. *A lot.* He made her feel trapped, like prey.

When she'd walked far enough away that the bon-fire was a glow in the distance and the roll of waves was all she could hear, the knot of tension in her neck loosened. She had gone the opposite direction of danger, and she stood in one of the spots where she felt safest, most at peace—the exposed reef. The ground under her feet shifted from sandy beach to rocky shelf. Tide pools were spread open to the moon. It was perfect, just her and the sea. She needed that, the peace she found there. She went toward a ledge of the reef where waves crashed and sprayed upward. Mussel shells jutted up like blunt black teeth. Slick sea lettuce and sea grasses hid crabs and unstable ground. She was barefoot, balancing on the edges of the reef, feeling that rush as the waves came ever closer, feeling herself fill up with the peace Dreadlocks had stolen.

Then she saw him standing in the surf in front of her, staring at her, oblivious to the waves that broke around him. "How did he get here first?"

She shivered, but then realized that it wasn't him. The guy was as defined as Dreadlocks, but he had long, loose, dark hair. *Just a surfer. Or Dreadlocks's friend.* The surfer wasn't wearing a wetsuit. He looked like he might be . . . naked. It was difficult to tell with the waves crashing around him; at the very least, he was topless in the frigid water.

He lifted his hand to beckon her closer, and she thought she heard him say, "I'm safe enough. Come talk to me."

It was her imagination, though. It had to be. She was just freaked out by Dreadlocks. There was no way this guy could've heard her over the breaking of waves, no way she could've heard him.

But that didn't change her suspicion that somehow they had just spoken.

Primal fear uncoiled in her belly, and for the second time that night, she backed away without looking. Her heel sliced open on the edge of a mussel shell. The sting of salt water made her wince as she walked farther away, unable to ignore the panic, the urge to run. She glanced back and saw that he hadn't moved, hadn't stopped watching her with that unwavering gaze. And her fear turned to fury.

Then she saw the long black leather coat slung carelessly on the sand; it looked like a darker version of the coat Dreadlocks had offered her. She stepped on it and ground her blood-and-sand-caked foot on it. It wasn't smooth like leather should be. Instead, the material under her foot was silk-soft fur, an animal's pelt, a seal's skin.

It *was* a pelt.

She pulled her gaze away from that dark pelt and stared at him. He still stood in the surf. Waves curled around him like the sea had formed arms of itself, hiding him, holding him.

He smiled again and told her, "Take it. It's yours now."

And she knew she had heard his voice that time; she'd *felt* the words on her skin like the wind that stirred the water. She didn't want to reach down, didn't want to lift that pelt into her arms, but she had no choice. Her bleeding foot had broken his glamour, ended his manipulation of her senses, and she knew him for what he truly was: a selchie. He was a fey creature, a seal person, and he wasn't supposed to exist.

Maybe it was fun to believe in them when she was a little girl sharing her storybooks with Nonny, but Alana knew that her grandmother's insistence that selchies were real was just another type of make-believe. Seals didn't walk on land among humans; they didn't slip out of their Other-Skins. They were just beautiful myths. She knew that—except she was looking at a selchie who was telling her to take his Other-Skin.

*Just like the one at the bonfire.*

She stood motionless as she tried to process the enormity of what had happened, what was happening right now.

*Two selchies. I met two freaking selchies . . . who tried to trap me.*

And in that instant, she understood: the fairy tales were all wrong. It wasn't the mortals' fault. Alana didn't want to stay there looking at him, but she was no longer acting of her own volition.

*I am trapped.*

The fishermen in the old stories who'd taken the selchies' pelts hadn't been entrapping innocent fey creatures: they'd been entrapped by selchie women. Perhaps it was too hard for the fishermen to admit that they were the ones who got trapped, but Alana suddenly knew the truth that none of the stories had shared. A mortal could no more resist the pull of that pelt than the sea could refuse to obey the pull of the moon. Once she took the pelt, lifted it into her mortal arms, she was bound to him. She knew what he was, knew the trap was sprung, but she was no different from the mortals in the stories she'd grown up hearing. She could not resist. She took the pelt and ran, hoping she could foist it off on someone else before he found her, before Murrin followed her home—because he had to be Murrin, the one Dreadlocks was talking about, the one that the creepy selchie had told her was *worse*.

Murrin watched her run, felt the irresistible need to follow her. She carried his skin with her: he had no choice but follow. It would have been better if she hadn't run.

With murmured epithets over her flight, he stepped out of the surf and made his way to the tiny caves the water had carved into the sandstone. Inside, he had his shore-clothes: woven sandals, well-worn jeans, a few shirts, and a timepiece. When his brother, Veikko, had gone ashore earlier, he'd borrowed the soft shirt Murrin had liked so. Instead, Murrin had to wear one that required fastening many small buttons. He hated buttons. Most of his family didn't go shore-walking often enough that they needed many clothes, but Murrin had been on land often enough that the lack of a decent shirt was displeasing. He barely fastened the shirt, slipping a couple of the tiny disks into the equally tiny holes, and went to find her—the girl he'd chosen over the sea.

He hadn't meant for her to find his Other-Skin like this, not yet, not now. He'd intended to talk to her, but as he was coming out of the water, he'd seen her—here and not at the party. He watched her, trying to figure how to walk out of the surf without startling her, but then he felt it: the touch of her skin on his pelt. His pelt wasn't to be there. It wasn't to happen like this. He'd had a plan.

A selchie couldn't have both a mate and the water, so Murrin had waited until he found a girl intriguing enough to hold his attention. After living with the moods of the sea, it wasn't an easy task to find a person worth losing the waves for.

*But I have.*

So he'd intended to ease her fears, to try to woo her instead of trapping her, but when she stepped on his Other-Skin, all of those choices had vanished. This was it: they were bound. Now, he was left doing the same thing his father had once done, trying to convince a mortal to trust him after he'd trapped her. The fact that *he* hadn't put his pelt where she'd find it didn't change anything. He was left trying to wait out her fears, to find a way to convince her to trust him, to hope for a way to persuade her to forgive him: all of the very same things he'd wanted to avoid.

Mortals weren't strong enough of will to refuse the enchantment that bound him to her. It wouldn't make her love him, but selchies grew up knowing that love wasn't often theirs to have. Tradition mattered more. Finding a mate, making a family, those mattered more.

And Murrin's plan to buck tradition by getting to know his intended first had gone horribly off course.

*Thanks to Veikko.*

At the dirty bathrooms along the beach parking lot, Alana saw a girl clad only in a thin top and ragged shorts. The girl was shivering, not that it was cold, but from something she'd shot up—or hadn't been able to shoot. Usually, the junkies and vagrants clustered in small groups, but this one was alone.

The pelt tingled and resumed looking again like a beautiful leather jacket as soon as Alana saw the girl. *Perfect.* Alana walked up and tried to hand it to the girl. "Here. You can use it to warm—"

But the girl backed away with something like horror on her face. She glanced from the coat to Alana's face, then out to the mostly empty lot. "I won't tell or anything. Please? Just—" She made a gagging noise and turned away.

Alana looked down. The pelt, still looking like a coat, was covered in blood. It was on her hands, her arms. Everywhere the seawater had been was now black-red in the glare of the streetlight. For a heartbeat, Alana thought she'd been wrong, that she'd hurt the selchie. She looked over her shoulder: a trail of almost perfectly tear-shaped droplets stretched behind her. Then, as she watched, those droplets shifted to a silvery-white, like someone had spilled mercury on the sand. They didn't sink. They balanced atop the sand, holding their shape. Alana glanced down and saw the blood on the coat shift to silver, too.

"See? It's fine. Just take it. It'll—"

The shivering girl had already gone.

" . . . be fine," Alana finished. She blinked back tears of frustration. "All I want is someone to hold out their arms so I can let go of it!"

With the same surety that told her what Murrin was, what Dreadlocks was, she realized that she couldn't cast the pelt away, but if someone was to reach for it, she could let go. It could fall to the ground, and then no one would be trapped. She just needed to find someone willing to reach out.

Twice more as she walked home she tried. Each time it was the same: people looked at her with terror or disgust as she held out what looked like a bloody coat. Only when they turned away did the dampness of the coat resume the appearance of thick, salty tears.

Whatever enchantment made her unable to resist taking the pelt was making it impossible to get rid of the thing, too. Alana thought about what she knew about selchies; her grandmother had told her stories of the seal people when Alana was a little girl: selchies, seal women, came to the shore. They slipped out of their Other-Skins, and sometimes, if they weren't careful, a fisherman or some random unmarried guy would find the skin and steal it. The new husbands hid the selchies' Other-Skins to keep their wives entrapped.

But Nonny hadn't said anything about male selchies; she also hadn't said that the seal women had entrapped the men. Nonny's stories made the selchies seem so sad, with their freedom to change to their seal shape stolen when their Other-Skins were hidden away. In the stories, the selchies were the victims; the humans were the villains—snatching helpless seal wives from the sea, tricking them, having power over them. The stories were all quite clear: the selchies were entrapped . . . but in the real world, Alana was the one feeling trapped.

By the time she reached her apartment, she was

wishing—yet again—that Nonny was still around to ask. She felt like a little kid missing her grandmother so badly, but Nonny was the Grown-up, the one who'd made everything better, while Mom was as clueless as Alana felt most days.

Outside her building, she paused. Their car was parked in the street alongside the building. Alana popped the trunk. Carefully, she folded the coat-pelt. After a furtive look around, she rubbed her face on the soft dark fur. Then, with a level of care she couldn't control, she tucked it under the spare blanket her mother kept in the trunk—part of the emergency kit for when they broke down. It felt as if there wasn't any other choice: she had to keep it safe, keep it out of his reach—and keep him out of others' reach.

*Protect my mate.* The words came unbidden— and very unwelcome—to her mind. She slammed the trunk and went to the front of the car. And as she did so often when she needed to be outside at night, she stretched out on the hood. It was still warm from the drive home from whatever party her mother'd been out to tonight.

Alana stared up at the moon and whispered, "Oh, Nonny, I'm so screwed."

Then, Alana waited. He'd come. She knew he would. And having to face him with her mom lurking around, gleeful that Alana'd brought home a guy . . . it would only make a bad scene worse.

*Better to do this outside.*

Murrin saw her reclined on a car reminiscent of the ones he'd seen parked by the beach for days on end. It was unsightly—covered in rust spots, one door handle missing. She, however, was lovely, long limbs and curved body. Short pelt-brown hair framed her sharp-angled face. When he'd seen her on the beach several good tides ago, he'd known she was the one: a girl who loved the reef and the moon was a treasure. The waiting had been awful, but he'd watched her habits and planned how to approach her. Things weren't going according to his plans, of course, but he'd find a way to make it work.

"Wife?" His heart sped at saying it, naming her, finally saying the word to her. He stepped closer to the car, not close enough to touch her, but closer still. After so many years dreaming of finding a wife, it was a heady thing to be so near her. It might not be how he'd imagined it, but it still *was.*

She sat up, her feet scraping against the car's hood. "What did you call me?"

"Wife." He approached her slowly, hands held out to the sides. No matter how many mortals he'd watched, or how many he'd met, he was unsure still. Obviously, calling her "wife" was not the right tactic. He tried again. "I don't know your other name yet."

"Alana. My *only* name is Alana." She moved so she was sitting with her legs folded to the side, in a posture typical of a selchie girl.

It was endearing. Her words weren't, though.

"I'm not your wife," she said.

"I am Murrin. Would you—"

"I'm not your wife," she repeated, slightly louder.

"Would you walk with me, Alana?" He loved the feel of her name—*Alana, my rock, my harbor, my Alana*—on his tongue.

But when he stepped closer, she tensed and stared at him with the same cautious expression she'd had on the beach. He liked that, her hesitation. Some of the mortals he'd met on the beach when he'd been in this form had been willing to lie down with him after only the briefest of words exchanged. It had been fun, but that wasn't what he wanted in a wife. The lack of meaning saddened him: he wanted every touch, each caress and sigh, to matter.

"Would you walk with me, Alana?" He ducked his head, causing his hair to fall forward, offering her as meek a posture as he could, trying to show that he wasn't a threat to her. "I would talk to you about *us*, so we can understand each other."

"Lanie?" An older version of his mate, obviously Alana's mother, stood with the light behind her. "Who's your friend?" She smiled at him. "I'm Susanne."

Murrin stepped toward Alana's mother. "I'm Murrin. I—"

"We were on our way out," Alana said. She grabbed his hand and pulled. "For tea."

"Tea? At this hour?" Alana's mother smiled, laughter playing under her expression. "Sure, baby. Just come home after the sun rises. We'll all sleep late tomorrow."

As they walked, Alana tried to think of what to say, but she found no words to start the conversation. She didn't want to ask him why she felt so drawn to him—or if it would get worse. She suspected that it was a result of whatever enchantment made her unable to give away his pelt. They were tied together. She got that part. She didn't want to know if he felt the same compulsion to reach out a hand and touch. But she knew resisting it took supreme effort.

*It's not real.* She glanced at him and her pulse sped. *It's not forever, either. I can get rid of him. I can. And I want to.*

She shoved her hands into her pockets and continued to walk silently beside him. Usually, the night felt too close when people—*well, just guys, actually*—were in her space. She didn't want to turn into her mom: believing in the next dreamer, chasing after the illusion that lust or neediness could evolve into something real. It didn't. *Ever.* Instead, the giddiness of the initial rush evolved into drama and tears every single time. It made more sense to end it before that inevitable and messy second stage. Short-term dating was cool, but Alana always abided by the Six-Week Rule: no one she couldn't ditch within or at six weeks. That meant she needed to find a way to extricate herself from Murrin within six weeks, and the only one who could help her figure out how was him.

At the old building that housed the coffee shop, he stopped.

Murrin glanced at her. "Is here good?"

"It's fine." Without meaning to, she pulled her hands out of her pockets and started to reach out. She scowled and crossed her arms over her chest. "It's not a date. I just didn't want you near my mother."

Silently, he reached out to open the door.

"What?" She knew she was surly, heard herself being mean. *And why shouldn't I? I didn't ask for this.*

He sighed. "I would sooner injure myself than harm your mother, Alana." He motioned for her to go inside. "Your happiness, your life, your family . . . these are what matter to me now."

"You don't know me."

He shrugged. "It is simply how things are."

"But . . ." She stared at him, trying to find words to argue, to make him . . . *what? Argue against trying to make me happy?* "This doesn't make sense."

"Come sit down. We'll talk." He walked to the far side

of the shop, away from the well-lit central space. "There's a table open here."

There were other empty tables, but she didn't point them out. She wanted privacy for their conversation. Asking him how to break some fairy-tale bond was weird enough; doing it with people listening was a bit too much.

Murrin stopped and pulled out her chair.

She sat down, trying not to be touched by his gentlemanly posture or seeming disregard for the girls—and a few guys—who were staring at him with blatant interest. He hadn't seemed to notice them, even when they stopped talking midsentence to smile up at him as he walked by their tables.

*And who could blame them for looking?* Alana might be unhappy being caught in this weird situation, but that didn't mean she wasn't just a little dazzled by how very luscious he was—not so much that she would want to stay with him, of course, but her heart sped every time she looked at him. *Pretty packages don't mean a thing. None of this matters. He* trapped *me.*

Murrin sat down in the chair across from her, watching her with an intensity that made her shiver.

"What do you want?" she asked.

He reached out and took her hand. "Do you not want to be here?"

"No. I don't want to be here *with you.*"

His voice was soothing as he asked, "So how can I please you? How do I make you want to be around me?"

"You can't. I want you to go away."

A series of unreadable expressions played over his face, too fleeting to identify, but he didn't reply. Instead, he gestured at the giant chalkboard that served as a menu and read off choices. "Mocha? Americano? Macchiato? Tea? Milk?"

She thought about pressing him for the answers she needed, but didn't. Hostility wasn't going to work. *Not yet.* Fighting wasn't going to get her answers, so she decided to try a different approach: reason. She took a steadying breath.

"Sure. Mocha. Double shot." She stood to reach into her jeans pocket for money.

He jumped up, managing to look far more graceful than anyone she'd ever met. "Anything with it?"

"No." She unfolded a five from the bills in her pocket and held it out. Instead of taking it, he scowled and stepped away from the table.

"Hold on." She shook the bill and held her hand farther out. "Take this."

He gave her another small scowl and shook his head. "I cannot."

"Fine. I'll get my own." She stepped around him.

With a speed that shouldn't have been possible, he

blocked her path; she stumbled briefly into him, steadying herself with a hand on his chest.

Sighing softly, he put a hand atop hers. "May I buy you a cup of coffee, Alana? Please? It doesn't indebt you to me or anything."

*Reason,* she reminded herself. *Refusing a cup of coffee is not reasonable.*

Mutely, she nodded and was rewarded with a warm look.

Once he walked away, she sat down and watched him wind through the crowd. He didn't seem fazed by the people jostling him or the crowded tables. He moved through the room easily, unnaturally so. Several times, he glanced at her and at the people seated around her— attentive without being possessive.

*Why does it matter?* She looked at him with an unfamiliar longing, knowing he wasn't really hers, knowing she didn't want to be tied to him but still feeling a strange wistfulness. *Is it a selchie thing?* She forced her gaze away and started thinking again of what to say, which questions to ask, how to undo the mess they were in.

A few minutes later, and again without any visible effort, Murrin moved through the crowd until he reached her, balancing two cups and a plate atop each one. The first plate had a thick sandwich; the second one was stacked high with brownies, cookies, and squares of chocolate. He handed her the mocha.

"Thank you," she murmured.

He nodded, sat down, and slid the plates to the center of the table between them. "I thought you might want to eat something."

She looked at the plate of desserts and the sandwich. "This is all for me?"

"I didn't know what you'd like best."

"You to leave," she said.

His expression was serious. "I can't do that. Please, Alana, you need to understand. This is how it's been for centuries. I didn't *intend* for you to be entrapped, but I can't walk away. I am not physically *able* to do so."

"Could you take it back? Your, umm, skin?" She held her breath.

He looked at her sadly again; his eyes seemed as wet-black as the sea at night. "If I find it where you've hidden it without you intending me to do so. Pure coincidence. Or if I'm angry enough to search after you've struck me three times. Yes, there are ways, but it's not likely. You can't help hiding it, and I can't search for it without cause."

Alana had suspected—*known*—it wasn't something she could easily escape, but she still needed to ask, to hear him tell her. She felt tears sting her eyes. "So what do we do?"

"We get to know each other. I hope you discover you want me to be near you. You hope I say something that helps you find a way to get rid of me." He sounded so sad when he said it that she felt guilty. "That, too, is how it's been for centuries."

The next hour passed in fits and starts of conversation. Periodically, Alana relaxed. Murrin could see that she was enjoying herself, but each time she noticed she was doing so, he saw a shadow of irritation flit over her face, and she put her walls back up. She swayed toward him, but then darted away from him. Hers was a strong will, and as much as he respected it, he despaired that her strength was set against him.

He watched the tilt of her head when she was listening; he heard the rhythm of her words when she spoke of her life on shore. He knew that it was a conscious machination—that she was assessing the situation in order to get free of him. But he had learned patience and flexibility in the sea. Those were skills that every selchie needed in order to survive. Murrin's father had warned that they were equally essential in relationships, and though Murrin hadn't thought he'd follow his father's way, he'd listened. Tonight he was glad he had.

Finally, the shop was empty of everyone but them, and Alana was yawning.

"You need to rest, Alana." He stood and waited for her. Her eyes were fatigue-heavy. Perhaps a good night's sleep would help them both.

She didn't look at him, but her guard was low enough that she accepted his hand—and gasped softly when she did.

Murrin froze, waiting for her to determine their next action. He had no answer, no clue how to respond. No one had warned him that the mere touch of her hand would evoke such a feeling: he'd fight until his last breath to keep her near him, to keep her safe, to make her happy. It was akin to the sea, this feeling that pulled at him. He'd drown under the weight of it, the enormity of it, and he'd not object as he did so.

Alana tried not to react to the feel of his hand in hers, but there was something *right* in the sensation; it was like feeling the universe snap into order. Peace, an always elusive sensation, was filling her. She found that on the reef, under the full moon, but it wasn't a feeling she experienced around people. She let go of his hand briefly—he didn't resist—and the feeling ebbed. But it was like watching the sea run away from her, seeing the water escape somewhere she couldn't follow. The water would flee even if she tried to grasp it, but unlike the sea, this felt like something almost tangible. She grabbed his hand and stared at their entwined fingers. *He was tangible.*

*And of the sea . . .*

She wondered if that was why she felt this way—

touching him was the same as touching the sea. She ran her thumb over his knuckles. His skin was no different than hers. *Now, at least.* The thought of him shifting into something else, something not-human, was almost enough to make her let go again. Almost.

"I won't hurt you, Alana." He was speaking then, murmuring words in a rhythmic way that was so very not-human.

She shivered. Her name had never sounded so beautiful. "People don't use names with every sentence."

He nodded, but his expression was guarded, carefully empty. "Would you prefer that I don't? I like your name, but I could—"

"Never mind. Just . . . I don't know. . . . I don't like this." She gestured at their hands, at him, and back at herself, but she held on to him as they left the coffee shop. She was so tired, so confused, and the only moment of peace she'd felt was when she'd touched his skin.

Once they were outside, she shifted topics again. "Where will you stay?"

"With you?"

She laughed before she could help herself. "Umm, I don't think so."

"I can't be too far from you now, Alana. Think of it as a leash. My reach only extends so far. I can sleep outside." He shrugged. "We don't exactly stay in houses most of the time. My mother does, but she's . . . like you. I stay with her some. It's softer, but it's not necessary."

Alana thought about it. She knew her mother wouldn't care: Susanne was utterly without what she liked to call "hang-ups," but it felt like admitting defeat to let him crash on her sofa. *So I tell him to sleep outside like an animal? He is an animal though, isn't he?* She paused; he stopped walking, too.

*What am I thinking to even consider letting him in my home?* He wasn't human, but an animal. Who knew what sort of rules he lived by—or if he even had rules or laws. She was no different from her mother: swayed by empty words, letting strange men into her haven. But he'd trapped her. And he wasn't the only one who'd tried. Something odd was happening, and she didn't like it. She let go of his hand and moved away from him.

"Who was the guy at the bonfire trying to give me his skin? Why were both of you . . . He said you were worse and . . ." She looked at him, at his face. "And why me?"

Murrin couldn't speak, couldn't process anything beyond the fact that his brother had tried to lure away his intended mate. He knew as soon as it happened that Veikko had taken Murrin's Other-Skin and laid it where Alana had found it, but he hadn't thought Veikko had approached her, too. *Why did he?* Veikko still had rare bursts of pique over Zoë's leaving, but they'd talked about it. *He said he understood . . . so why was he speaking with my Alana?*

Murrin wondered if he ought to assure Veikko that Alana would be safe, that she was not like Zoë, that she would not be lost in a potentially fatal depression. *Perhaps he was trying to protect Alana? And me?* That would make more sense to Murrin, but for the almost certain fact that Veikko had been responsible for putting Murrin's Other-Skin in Alana's path. No other selchies had been on the shore.

*None of this makes sense . . . nor is it something to share now.*

It was far more complicated than Alana needed to deal with on top of everything else, so Murrin quashed his confusion and suspicions and said, "Veikko is my brother."

"Your brother?"

Murrin nodded.

"He scared me." She blushed when she said it, as if fear were something to be ashamed of, but the open admission was only a blink. Alana was still angry. Her posture was tense: hands clenched, spine straight, eyes narrowed. "He said you were worse, and that he'd be back. He—"

"Veikko—Vic—is a bit outdated in his interactions with . . . humans." Murrin hated having to use the word, but it was unavoidable. He was not what she was, would never be what she was. It was something they needed to acknowledge. Murrin stepped closer. Despite her anger, she was in need of comfort.

"Why did he say you were worse?"

"Because I wanted to get to know you before I told you what I was. None of this was intentional. My Other-Skin was . . ." He paused, considered telling her that he suspected that Veikko had entrapped her, and decided against it. There were many years in which Alana and Veikko would be forced to be near each other: with a simple omission, the strife of her resenting him was avoidable. "It was not to be there. *You* were not to be there. I was coming to meet you, to try to date you as humans do."

"Oh." She crossed her arms over her chest. "But . . ."

"Vic thinks I am 'worse' than others in my family because I am going against tradition . . . or was hoping to." He gave her a sheepish smile. "He thinks it is worse that I would try to court you and then reveal myself. Not that it matters now. . . ."

"How is that worse?"

"I've been asking that question for years." He held out his hand. "It is not what I will teach my children . . . one day when I become a father. It is not what I wanted, but we are together now. We'll work it out."

She took his outstretched hand in hers. "We don't have to stay together."

He didn't answer, *couldn't* answer for a moment. Then he said, "I'm sorry."

"Me, too. I don't do relationships, Murrin." Her fingertips stroked his hand absently.

"I didn't mean to trap you, but I'm not eager to let go, either." He expected her to argue, to grow angry, but like the sea, her moods weren't quite what he anticipated.

She smiled then, not like she was unhappy, but like she was dangerous. "So I guess I need to convince you then."

*She really is perfect for me.*

Over the next three weeks, little by little, Alana's doubts were replaced by a tentative friendship. *It doesn't hurt to be nice to him. It's not his fault.* She started telling herself that they could be friends. Even if she couldn't get rid of him, she didn't necessarily need to *date* him, and she definitely didn't need to *marry* him.

One night, she woke with a start in the middle of the night, shivering and thinking of Murrin. They were friends. Okay, he was crashing on her sofa, and he did share her meals, but that wasn't a commitment. It was practicality. He had nowhere to go. He couldn't sleep on the beach. And he bought the groceries, so he wasn't mooching. He was just . . . a good friend who was always there.

*And he makes me happy.*

She went into the living room. Murrin was standing in front of the window, eyes closed, face upturned. The expression on his face was one of pain. She was beside him before she'd thought twice about it.

"Murrin?"

He turned and looked at her. The longing in his eyes was heartstoppingly awful, but he blinked and it was gone. "Are you ill?"

"No." She took his hand and led him away from the window. "Are *you*?"

"Of course not." He smiled, and it would've been reassuring if she hadn't seen the sadness still lingering in his eyes.

"So, what's up?"

"Nothing." He gestured toward her bedroom doorway. "Go ahead. I'm good."

She thought about it, about him being away from his family, his home, everything familiar. All they talked about was what she wanted, what made her happy, how she felt. *He* had just as much upheaval, more even. "Talk to me. We're trying to be friends, right?"

"Friends," he repeated. "Is that what we are going to be?"

And she paused. Despite the weirdness, she wasn't feeling uncomfortable anymore. She touched his cheek and let her hand linger there. He was a good person.

She said, "I'm not trying to be difficult."

"Nor am I." He leaned his face into the palm of her hand. "But . . . I'm trying to be careful."

She put her hands on his shoulders and went up on her tiptoes. The touch of her hand against his skin was enough to make the world settle into that wondrous sense of completion that it always did. Over the last couple of days, she'd let her fingertips brush against his arm, bumped her shoulder into him—little touches to see if it was always so perfect. It was. Her heart was racing now though.

He didn't move.

"No promises," she whispered, and then she kissed him—and that feeling of bliss that she'd brushed with every touch of his skin consumed her. She couldn't breathe, move, anything but feel.

Murrin watched Alana warily the next day. He wasn't sure what had happened, if it meant anything or if she was just feeling sympathy. She'd been very clear in her insistences that they were friends, *just* friends, and that friends was all they ever could be. He waited, but she didn't mention the kiss—and she didn't repeat it.

*Perhaps it was a fluke.*

For two more days, she acted as she had before The Kiss: she was kind, friendly, and sometimes brushed against him as if it were an accident. It never was; he knew that. Still, she didn't do anything out of the ordinary.

On the third day, she flopped down next to him

on the sofa. Susanne was out at a yoga class—not that it would've mattered. Susanne seemed inordinately pleased that Alana wanted him to stay with them; Murrin suspected Susanne wouldn't object to him sharing Alana's room. It was Alana who set the boundaries—the same Alana who was currently sitting very close, staring at him with a bemused smile.

"I thought you liked kissing me the other night," she said.

"I did."

"So . . ."

"I don't think I understand."

"We can *pretend* what we are is friends . . . but we're dating. Right?" She toyed with the edge of her shirt.

He waited for several breaths, but she didn't say anything else. So he asked, "What about your plan to convince me to leave?"

"I'm not sure any more." She looked sheepish. "I can't promise forever, or truthfully, next month, but I think about you all the time. I'm happier around you than I've ever been in my life. There's something . . . magical when we touch. I know it's not real, but . . ."

"It's not real?" he repeated.

"It's a selchie thing, right? Like the urge to pick up the Other-Skin." She paused. Her next words came out in a rush. "Does it work both ways?"

She was close enough that it would be only natural to

pull her into his arms. So he did. He lifted her onto his lap and threaded his fingers through her hair. He let the tendrils tangle around his fingers.

"It's not a selchie thing at all," he told her, "but it does flow both ways."

She started to pull back. "I thought it was just . . . you know . . . a magic thing."

He cradled her head in his hand, holding her close, and said, "It *is* magic. Finding a mate, falling in love, seeing her love you back? That's real magic."

And his Alana, his mate, his perfect match didn't move away. She leaned close enough to kiss . . . not in sympathy or misplaced emotion, but in affection.

*Everything is perfect.* He wrapped his arms more securely around her and knew that, despite his inability to court her before they were bound, it was all going to be fine. She hadn't said the words, but she loved him.

*My Alana, my mate . . .*

The next evening, Murrin took the bag of pearls to the jeweler his family had always gone to see. Davis Jewels closed in a few minutes, but the jewel man and his wife never objected to Murrin's visits. Mr. Davis smiled when Murrin walked in. "Let me ring Madeline, and tell her I'll be late."

Mr. Davis went to the door, locked it, and set the security system. If Murrin closed his eyes, he could watch the older man's steps in his memory, and they'd not vary from what was happening in front of him.

When Mr. Davis went to call his wife, Murrin waited at the counter. He unfolded the cloth he carried for such trips and tipped the bag's contents on to the smooth material.

Mr. Davis finished his call and opened his mouth to speak, but whatever he'd intended to say fled when he looked at the counter. He walked over, glancing only briefly at Murrin, attention fixed on the pearls. "You've never brought this many...."

"I need to make a purchase as well this time." Murrin gestured at the glass cases in the store. "I am ... marrying."

"That's why the necklace. I wondered." Mr. Davis smiled, his face crinkling into a maze of lines as thick as the fronds of kelp, beautiful in his aging skin. Here was a man who understood love: Mr. Davis and his wife still looked at each other with a glow in their eyes.

He went in the back of the store and brought out a case with the pearl necklace. It was strung with pearls Murrin had selected over many years.

*For Alana.*

Murrin opened it and ran his fingertip over them. "Perfect."

Mr. Davis smiled again, then he took the pearls from the cloth over to his table to examine them. After years of buying pearls from Murrin's family, the man's examination of the pearls—studying their size, shape, color, and lustre—was cursory, but still a part of the process.

The order of the jeweler's steps was as familiar as the currents to Murrin. Usually, he waited motionless while the man went about his routine. This time, he stared into the display cases.

When Mr. Davis came over, Murrin gestured at the rows of solitary stones on plain bands. "Help me select one of those?"

The jeweler told Murrin how much he'd pay for the pearls and added, "I don't know how much of that you want to spend."

Murrin shrugged. "I want my wife to be pleased. That is all that matters."

Alana wasn't surprised to see Dreadlocks—*Vic*—leaning on a wall outside the coffee shop where she'd been waiting while Murrin was off on a secret errand. She'd thought she'd seen Vic several times lately. She didn't stop though. She wasn't sure she knew what to say to him. When she'd seen him watching, she thought to ask Murrin about him, but she wasn't sure what to say or ask.

Vic matched his pace to hers and walked alongside her. "Would you hear what I have to say, Alana?"

"Why?"

"Because you are mated to my brother, and I am worried about him."

"Murrin doesn't seem like he's very close to you . . . and he's fine. Happy." She felt a tightness in her chest, a panic. It was so unlike what she felt when she was with Murrin.

"So you haven't seen him watching the sea? He doesn't ache for it?" Vic's expression was telling: he knew the answer already. "He can't admit it. It's part of the . . . enchantment. You trapped him here when you stole his Other-Skin. He can't tell you he's unhappy, but you'll see it in time. He'll grow miserable, hate you. One day you'll see him staring out to sea . . . maybe not yet, but we can't help it."

Alana thought about it. She *had* seen Murrin late at night when he thought she was asleep. He'd been staring into the distance, facing the direction of the water, even though he couldn't see it from the apartment. The look of longing on his face was heartrending.

"He's going to resent you in time. We always do." Vic's mouth curled in a sardonic smile. "Just as you resent us. . . ."

"I don't resent Murrin," she started.

"Not now, perhaps. You did though." Vic toyed with one long green strand of his hair. "You resented him for trapping you. It's a cruel fate to be trapped. My mate resented me, too. Zoë . . . that was her name. My Zoë . . ."

"Was?"

"I suspect it still is." He paused, a pensive look on his face. "But in time, we resent you. *You* keep us from what we deserve: our freedom. I didn't want to be angry with my Zoë. . . ."

Alana thought about Murrin being trapped, being angry at her, resenting her for keeping him landbound. The bitterness in Vic's eyes wasn't something she wanted to see in Murrin's gaze.

"So what should I do?" she whispered.

"A mortal can't be tied to two selchies . . . just lift up my skin. Murrin will be free then."

"Why would you do that? We'd be—" Alana tried not to shudder at the thought of being bound to Vic. "I don't want to be your . . . anything."

"Not your type?" He stepped closer, as predatory and beautiful as he had looked at the party when they first met. "Aaah, Alana, I feel badly that I bungled things when I met you. I want to help Murrin as my brother helped me. If not for him, Zoë and I would still be . . . trapped. I'd be kept from the sea. Murrin unbound us."

"It's cool that you want to help him, but *I don't want to be with you.*" She repressed another shudder at that thought, but only barely.

Vic nodded. "We can work around that detail. I won't ask what Murrin has of you . . . I don't seek a wife. I need to fix things, though. Maybe I didn't know the right words when we met. I can't say I have the kind of *experience* that Murrin has with mortal girls, but . . ."

Alana froze. "What do you mean?"

"Come now, Alana. We aren't exactly built for faithfulness. Look at us." Veikko gestured at himself. That self-assured look was back. "Mortals don't exactly tell us *no*. The things you feel when you see us . . . hundreds of girls . . . not that he's been with every one of them . . . What you feel is instinct. It's not really *love*; it's just a reaction to pheromones."

Alana struggled between jealousy and acceptance. Vic wasn't telling her anything that she hadn't thought. In some ways it was just an extreme version of the logic behind the Six-Week Rule.

"I *owe* him this," Vic was saying. "And you don't really think you love him, do you?"

She didn't cry, but she wanted to. She hadn't said those words to Murrin, not yet, but she'd thought about it. She'd felt it. *Am I a fool? Is any of it real?*

She'd asked Murrin, but was he telling the truth? Did it even matter? If Murrin would hate her in time, she should let him go now. She didn't want that between them.

If Vic was telling the truth, there was no reason to keep Murrin with her, and plenty of reasons to let him go. *Soon.* He wasn't hers to keep. He wasn't really hers at all. *It's a trick.* He belonged to the sea, and with that came relationships, fleeting relationships, with other girls. *Is the way I feel a lie, or is Vic lying?* It made more sense that Vic was telling her the truth: people didn't fall in love this quickly; they didn't break all of their rules so easily. *It's just the selchie thing.* She forced her thoughts away from the roiling mix of emotions and took several calming breaths. "So how do we do it?"

Murrin found Alana sitting at the reef, but she wasn't happy. She looked like she'd been weeping.

"Hey." She glanced at him only briefly.

"Are you okay?" He didn't want to pry too much: her acceptance of him in her life still felt tenuous.

Instead of answering, she held out a hand to him.

He sat behind her, and she leaned back into his embrace. The waves rolled over the exposed reef and up to the rocky ledge where they were sitting. He sighed at the touch of the briny water. *Home.* He couldn't have imagined being this content: his Alana and his water both against his skin.

*Perfection . . . except that Alana seems sad.*

"I didn't expect . . . to care, especially so soon. I want you to be happy," she said. "Even if it's not real—"

"It *is* real." He took out the pearl necklace and draped it around Alana's throat. "And I am happy."

She gasped softly and ran her fingertips over the

pearls. "I can't—" She shook her head. "Do you miss it?"

"The sea? It's right here."

"But do you miss . . . changing and going out there? Meeting other people?" She tensed in his arms.

"I'm not going to leave you," he consoled. His mother had often looked at the sea as if it was an enemy who'd steal away her family if she wasn't careful. That wasn't what he wanted. He wrapped his arms around her again. "I am right where I need to be."

She nodded, but he could feel her tears falling on his hands.

Alana thought about it and decided that trusting Vic completely was foolish. He was right: she needed to let Murrin go before he resented her for keeping him from the sea. Murrin wasn't thinking clearly. Whatever enchantment made him need to stay close to her was keeping him from admitting that he longed for the sea. If he went back . . . there were selchies he could meet. None of that meant that she wanted to risk being tied to Vic— so she opted to try a plan she'd come up with before, but had rejected as too dangerous.

*And unnecessary because love took over.*

He was sleeping when she left the apartment. She thought about kissing him goodbye, but knew that would wake him.

She let the door close behind her; then she went

silently to the street and popped the trunk of the car. It was in there, his pelt. It was a part of him as surely as the seemingly human skin she'd caressed when he sat beside her late at night watching old movies with the sound down low. Gently, she gathered the pelt to her, trying not to wonder at how warm it was, and then she ran.

There weren't tears in her eyes. *Yet.* She'd have time enough for that later. First she had to focus on getting to the beach before he realized what she was doing. She ran through the streets in the not-yet-light day. The sunrise wasn't too far off, but it was early enough that the surfers hadn't started arriving yet.

She knew he'd come soon. He had to follow the pull of his pelt when it was in her hands, but knowing didn't make it any easier to hurry. She felt an urgency to get done with it before he arrived, but she felt a simultaneous despair.

*It's for the best.*

She waded into the surf. Waves tugged at her, like strange creatures butting at her knees to pull her under the surface; kelp slid over her bare skin, slithering lengths that made her pulse race too fast.

*It's the right thing for both of us.*

He was there then. She heard Murrin calling her name. "Alana! Stop!"

*In the end, we'll both be miserable if I don't.*

The pelt was heavy in her arms; her fingers clutched at it.

He was beside her. "Don't—"

She didn't hear the rest. She let the waves take her legs out from under her. She closed her eyes and waited. The instinct to survive outweighed any enchantment, and her arms released the pelt so she could swim.

Beside her, she felt him, his silk-soft fur brushing against her as his selchie pelt transformed his human body into a sleek-skinned seal. She slid her hand over his skin, and then she swam away from him, away from the wide open sea where he was headed.

*Goodbye.*

She wasn't sure if it was the sea or her tears, but she could taste salt on her lips as she surfaced.

When she stood on the beach again, she could see him in the distance, too far away to hear her voice if she gave in and asked him to come back. She wouldn't. A relationship based on enchantment was ill-fated from the beginning. It wasn't what she wanted for either of them. She knew that, was certain of it, but it didn't ease the ache she felt at his absence.

*I don't really love him. It's just leftover magic.*

She saw Vic watching her from the shore. He said something she couldn't hear over the waves, and then he was gone, too. They were both gone, and she was left reminding herself that it was better this way, that what she'd felt hadn't been real.

*So why does it hurt so bad?*

For several weeks, Murrin watched her, his Alana, his mate-no-more, on the shore that was his home-no-more. He didn't know what to do. She'd rejected him, cast him back to the sea, but she seemed to mourn it.

*If she didn't love me, why does she weep?*

Then one day, he saw that she was holding the pearls he'd given her. She sat on the sand, running the strand through her fingers, carefully, lovingly. All the while, she wept.

He came to shore there at the reef where he'd first chosen her, where he'd watched her habits to try to find the best way to woo her. It was more difficult this time, knowing that she knew so many of his secrets and found him lacking. At the edge of the reef, he slid out of his Other-Skin and tucked it in a hollow under an edge of the reef where it would be hidden from sight. Giant sea stars clung to the underside of the reef ledge, and he wondered if she'd seen them. His first thoughts were too often still of her, her interests, her laughter, her soft skin.

She didn't hear his approach. He walked up to stand beside her and asked the question that had been plaguing him. "Why are you sad?"

"Murrin?" She stuffed the necklace into her pocket

and backed away, careful to look where she stepped, no doubt looking for his Other-Skin, then glancing back at him after each step. "I set you free. Go away. Go on."

"No." He had dreamed of being this close to her ever since he'd been forced away from her. He couldn't help it; he smiled.

"Where is it?" she asked, her gaze still darting frantically around the exposed tide pools.

"Do you want me to show—"

"*No.*" She crossed her arms over her chest and scowled. "I don't want to do that again."

"It's hidden. You won't touch it unless you let me lead you to it." He walked closer then, and she didn't back away this time—nor did she approach him as he'd hoped.

"You're, umm, naked." She blushed and turned away. She picked up her backpack and pulled out one of the warm hoodies and jeans she'd found at the thrift store when they were shopping that first week. She shoved them at him. "Here."

Immeasurably pleased that she carried his clothes with her—surely that meant she hoped he'd return—he got dressed. "Walk with me?"

She nodded.

They walked for a few steps, and she said, "You have no reason to be here. I broke the spell or whatever. You don't need—"

"What spell?"

"The one that made you have to stay with me. Vic explained it to me. You can go get with a seal girl now. . . . It's what's best."

"Vic explained it?" he repeated. Veikko had convinced Alana to risk her life to get rid of Murrin. It made his pulse thud as it did when he rode the waves during a storm. "And you believed him *why*?"

Her cheeks reddened again.

"What did he tell you?"

"That you'd resent me because you lost the sea, and that you couldn't tell me, and that what I felt was just pheromones . . . like the hundreds of other girls you . . ." She blushed brighter still. "And I saw you at night, Murrin. You looked so sad."

"Now I am sad in the waves watching you." He pulled her closer, folding her into his arms, kissing her as they'd kissed only a few times before.

"I don't understand." She touched her lips with her fingertips, as if there were something odd about his kissing her. "Why?"

Even the thriving reefs weren't as breathtakingly beautiful as she was as she stood there with kiss-swollen lips and a wide-eyed gaze. He kept her in his arms, where she belonged, where he wanted her always to be, and told her, "Because I love you. That's how we express—"

"No. I mean, you don't *have* to love me now. I freed

you." Her voice was soft, a whisper under the wind from the water.

"I never had to *love* you. I just had to stay with you unless I reclaimed my skin. If I wanted to leave, I'd have found it in time."

Alana watched him with a familiar wariness, but this time there was a new feeling—hope.

"Vic lied because I'd helped his mate leave him. She was sick. He was out with mortal girls constantly . . . and she was trapped and miserable." Murrin glanced away, looking embarrassed. "Our family doesn't know. Well, they might suspect, but Veikko never told them because he'd need to admit his cruelty, too. I thought he'd forgiven me. He said . . ."

"What?"

"He is my brother. I trusted him. . . ."

"I did, too." She leaned closer and wrapped her arms around him. "I'm sorry."

"Sooner or later, we will need to deal with him." Murrin sounded both sad and reluctant. "But in the meantime, if he talks to you—"

"I'll tell you."

"No more secrets," he said. Then he kissed her.

His lips tasted like the sea. She closed her eyes and let herself enjoy the feel of his hands on her skin, gave in to the temptation to run her hands over his chest. It was the same heady feeling she dreamt about most every night since he'd gone. Her pulse thrummed like the crash of waves behind her as he moved to kiss her neck.

*He's mine. He loves me. We can—*

"My beautiful wife," he whispered against her skin.

With more than a little reluctance, she stepped away from him. "We could try things a little differently this time, you know. Go slower. I want you here, but being married at my age isn't good. I have plans . . ."

"To see other people?"

"No. Not at all." She sat down on the sand. When he didn't move, she reached for his hand and tugged until he sat beside her. Then she said, "I don't want to see other people, but I'm not ready to be married. I'm not even done with high school." She glanced over at him. "I missed you all the time, but I don't want to lose me to have you. And I want you to be *you*, too. . . . Did you miss changing?"

"I did, but it'll get easier. This is how things are."

Murrin sounded so calm, and while Alana knew that Vic had lied about a lot of things, she also knew this was something he hadn't needed to lie about. She hadn't imagined the sadness she'd seen on Murrin's face when she'd seen him staring toward the water.

She asked, "But what if you could still have the sea? We could . . . date. You could still be who you are. I could still go to school and, umm, college."

"You'd be only mine? But I get to keep the sea?"

She laughed at his suspicious tone. "You do know that the sea isn't the same as being with another girl, right?"

"Where's the sacrifice?"

"There isn't one. There's patience, trust, and not giving up who we are." She leaned into his embrace, where she could find the same peace and pleasure the sea had always held for her.

*How could I have thought it was better to be apart?*

He smiled then. "We get each other. I get the sea, and you have to go to school? It sounds like I get everything, and you . . ."

"I do, too. You *and* time to do the things I need to so I can have a career someday."

She had broken her Six-Week Rule, but having a relationship didn't have to mean giving up on having a future. With Murrin, she could have both.

He reached over and pulled the pearls out of her pocket. With a solemn look, he fastened them around her throat. "I love you."

She kissed him, just a quick touch of lips, and said it back. "I love you, too."

"No Other-Skin, no enchantments," he reminded her.

"Just us," she said.

And that was the best sort of magic.